A shaken Dr Harold W. Smith awaited Remo at the hotel.

'I can't be seen here with you. Not even in the same hotel. With the lunatic assassination theories and committees running around, they could easily turn over a rock and find all of us.'

'What's the problem, other than you've lost your sense of reason?' Remo chided.

'The problem is the President of the United States is going to be assassinated. I don't have the time to go into how, I am sure of it, but you know we have our sources and our calculations.'

'So the President's going to be killed. So what?' Remo said.

'Have you seen the Vice President?' Smith said.

'We've got to save the President,' Remo said.

'We have to, but not for that reason. This country is so weak we can't afford to lose another President. We're trying to convince the President that his life is in danger, but he says it's up to God. You've got to convince him.'

Remo and Chiun would have to call on other gods to save the United States from anarchy.

Also by Richard Sapir and Warren Murphy

and published by Corgi Books

Richard Sapir and
Warren Murphy

The Destroyer 31:
THE HEAD MEN

CORGI BOOKS
A DIVISION OF TRANSWORLD PUBLISHERS LTD

THE DESTROYER 31: THE HEAD MEN

A CORGI BOOK 0 552 11127 9

First publication in Great Britain

Published by arrangement with Pinnacle Books Inc.
275 Madison Avenue, New York, N.Y. 10016, U.S.A.

PRINTING HISTORY
Corgi edition published 1979
Copyright © 1974 by Richard Sapir and Warren Murphy

Corgi Books are published by Transworld Publishers Ltd
Century House, 61-63 Uxbridge Road,
Ealing, London W.5.
Made and printed in Great Britain by
William Collins Sons & Co Ltd, Glasgow

For the most unique Charley I know, and for the glorious House of Sinanju, P.O. Box 1149, Pittsfield, Massachusetts.

THE HEAD MEN

CHAPTER ONE

This death threat made him think.

It had that real quality about it, as if it weren't so much a threat as a promise.

The caller had sounded so much like an authentic businessman that Ernest Walgreen's secretary had put him right through.

"It's a Mr. Jones."

"What does he want?" asked Walgreen. As president of DataComputronics in Minneapolis, Minnesota, he had learned to rely on his secretary, so much so that when he met people at business functions he would instinctively look for her to tell him which person he should warm up to and which he shouldn't. It was a simple question of not bothering to use his own judgment because his secretary's had proved so much better over the years.

"I don't know, Mr. Walgreen. He sounded like you were expecting his call. He says it's a somewhat private matter."

"Put him on," Walgreen said. He could work while he talked, reading proposals, checking out contracts, signing documents. It was an executive's attribute, a mind that could be in two

1

places at once. His father had had it; his own son did not.

Walgreen's grandfather had been a farmer and his father had owned a drugstore. Walgreen had thought there was a natural progression, from farm to pharmacy to executive suite, and on to possibly president of a university or perhaps the clergy. But, no, his own son had bought a small farm and had returned to growing wheat and worrying about the frequency of the rains and the price of crops.

Ernest Walgreen had thought the progress of the Walgreen family was a ladder, not a circle. There were worse things than farming, but few that were harder, he thought. But he knew it would be of no avail to argue with his son. The Walgreens were stubborn and made up their own minds. Grandpa Walgreen had once said, "The purpose of trying is trying. It ain't so damned important to get somewhere as it is to be on your way."

Young Ernest had asked his father what that meant. His father said, "Grandpa means it isn't how you put it in the bottle, but what you put in."

Years later Walgreen realized that that was just a simple contradiction of what Grandpa had said, but by then he didn't have too much time to think about it. He was too busy, and before Grandpa died he commended Ernest Walgreen for using his very modest skills, "to become one of the richest little pissers in the whole damned state. I didn't think you had it in you." Grandpa Walgreen talked like that. All the Walgreens made up their own minds.

"Mr. Walgreen, we're going to kill you," came

the voice over the telephone. It was a man. A steady voice. It was not the usual sort of threat.

Walgreen knew threats. His first ten years out of the university were spent guarding President Truman in the Secret Service, a career which, despite its promised promotions for one as bright and thorough as Walgreen, did not go as far up the ladder as Walgreen had intended to take himself and his family. But because of that he knew threats and he knew most of them were made by people who couldn't carry out real physical harm on their targets. The threat itself was the attack.

Most of the real dangers came from people who never sent any threat at all. The Secret Service still checked out the threateners and had them watched, but it was not so much to protect the President as to protect the department in the unlikely event that a threatener actually went out and tried to do something about his hatred. Eighty-seven percent of all recorded death threats made in America over a year were made by drunks. Less than three-hundredth's of one percent of those threats ever resulted in anything.

"You just threatened my life, didn't you?" said Walgreen. He put aside the pile of contracts and his desk, wrote down the time of the call, and buzzed his secretary to listen in.

"Yes, I did."

"May I ask why?"

"Don't you want to know when?" said the voice. It had a twang, but it was not midwest. Walgreen placed it somewhere east of Ohio and south. Virginia in the west, possibly. The voice sounded in the late forties. It was raspy. Walgreen wrote down on a small white pad: *11:03*

3

a.m., twangy voice, South. Virginia? Male. Raspy.
Probably a smoker. Late forties.

"Certainly I want to know when, but more than that I want to know why."

"You wouldn't understand."

"Try me," said Walgreen.

"In due time. What are you going to do about this?"

"I'm going to report it to the police."

"Good. And what else?"

"I'll do whatever the police tell me."

"Not enough, Mr. Walgreen. Now you're a rich man. You should be able to do more than just phone the police."

"Do you want money?"

"Mr. Walgreen, I know you want to keep me talking. But I also know that even if the police were sitting in your lap, you would not be able to trace this call in less than three minutes . . . and considering they are not, the real talking time is closer to eighteen minutes before you could trace this call."

"I don't get death threats every day."

"You used to. You dealt with them all the time. For money, remember?"

"What do you mean?" asked Walgreen, knowing exactly what the caller meant. The caller knew Walgreen had worked for the Secret Service, but even more important knew exactly what Walgreen's job had been. Even his wife didn't know that.

"You know what I mean, Mr. Walgreen."

"No, I don't."

"Where you used to work. Now, don't you think you could provide yourself some good pro-

4

tection with all your friends at the Secret Service and with all your money?"

"All right. If you insist, I'll protect myself. Then what?"

"Then we'll kill your ass anyway, Ernie. Hahaha."

The caller hung up. Ernest Walgreen wrote down the last note on the sheet. *11:07.* The caller had spoken for four minutes.

"Wow," said Walgreen's secretary, bursting into the office. "I got down every word he said. Do you think he's for real?"

"Very," said Ernest Walgreen. He was fifty-four years old and he felt drained that day. It was as if something in him were crying about the injustice of it. As if there were better times for death threats, not when his son's wife was about to give birth, not when he had bought the ski lodge in Sun Valley, Utah, not when the company he had founded was about to have a record year, not when Mildred, his wife, had just found a consuming hobby of pottery that made her even more cheerful. These were the best years of his life and he found himself telling himself that he was sorry this threat didn't come when he was young and poor. He found himself thinking, *I'm too rich to die now. Why didn't the bastards do it when I had trouble with the mortgage payments?*

"What should I do?" asked his secretary.

"Well, for the time being, we'll move you down the hall. Who knows what these lunatics will do and there's no point getting anyone killed who doesn't have to be."

"You think they're lunatics?"

5

"No," said Walgreen. "That's why I want you to move several offices away."

To his sorrow, the police also thought it was a call by a lunatic. The police gave him a lecture that came right out of a Secret Service manual on terrorists. Worse, it was a dated manual.

The police captain was named Lapointe. He was roughly Walgreen's age. But where Walgreen was lean and tanned and neat, Lapointe's fleshy expanse seemed held together only by his uniform. He had condescended to see Walgreen because Walgreen was an important businessman. He spoke to Walgreen as if addressing a ladies' tea on the horrors of crime.

"What you've got is your lunatic terrorist, unafraid to die," he said.

"That's wrong," Walgreen said. "They all say they're willing to die, but that's not the case."

"The manual says it is."

"You are referring to an old Secret Service manual which was acknowledged as incorrect almost as soon as it came out."

"I hear it all the time. Just on television, a commentator said terrorists aren't afraid to die. I heard it."

"It's still wrong. And I don't think I am dealing with a terrorist."

"The terrorist mind is cunning."

"Captain Lapointe, what I want to know is what are you going to do for the protection of my life?"

"We're going to give you thorough police protection, weave a defense web around you on one hand and try to identify and immobilize the terrorist in his lair on the other hand."

"You still haven't said what you are going to do."

"I most certainly have," said Lapointe, harumphing indignantly.

"Be specific," said Walgreen.

"You wouldn't understand."

"Try me," said Walgreen.

"It's very technical," warned Captain Lapointe.

"Go ahead."

"First we pull files looking for an MO, which is . . ."

"Which is modus operandi and you're going to find out all the people in this area who have phoned other people threatening to kill them, and you're going to ask them where they were at 11:03 today and when you find a few who give funny or contradictory stories, you will annoy them until they tell you something that the city attorney is willing to prosecute on. Meanwhile, the people who are going to kill me will have killed me."

"That's very negative."

"Captain Lapointe, I don't think these people are in your files. What I would like is a team surveillance and some access to people who know how to use weapons. With luck, we might foil the first attempt on my life and be able to find out possibly who the killers are. I think it's more than one which gives them more power but also makes them more liable to exposure, especially at their linkages."

"Secondly," said Lapointe, "we're going to send out an all points bulletin . . . that's an APB . . ."

Walgreen was out of Lapointe's office before the sentence was finished. No help there, he thought.

7

At home he told his wife he was going to Washington. Mildred was at her small Shim-oo pottery wheel. She was centering a reddish mound of clay and the spring heat had given her skin a healthy flush.

"You've never looked so beautiful, dear."

"Oh, c'mon. I'm a mess," she said. But she laughed.

"There isn't a day that goes by that I don't think more and more how right I was to marry you. How lucky I was."

And she smiled again and in that smile there was so much life that the great death he knew he was facing, made no less great by its commonness to all men, was, in that smile of life, made less fearful for a moment.

"I married a beautiful person too, Ernie."

"Not as beautiful as I did."

"I think so, dear. I think so."

"You know," he said, trying to be casual but not so casual that Mildred would see the effort and suspect something, "I can finish up a Washington project in three weeks, if . . ."

"If I got away on a trip," she said.

"Yes," said Walgreen. "Maybe to your brother's in New Hampshire."

"I was thinking of Japan."

"Maybe we'll both go, but after your brother's."

She left without finishing the pot. It would be two days before he found she had spoken with his secretary and knew how seriously he had taken that telephone threat. He would realize later she knew why she was being sent away and did not let on so he would not carry the extra burden of worry. When he did realize it would be too late.

She took an afternoon flight to New Hampshire and the last picture Ernest Walgreen would remember of his wife was how she fumbled with her purse for her ticket, as she had fumbled with her purses since he had met her so very long ago when they were young together, as they had remained until that airport, young together, always.

At Secret Service headquarters in Washington, when Ernest Walgreen got through the lower functionaries to finally speak with a district man, he was greeted by:

"Well, here comes the big rich businessman. How ya' doing Ernie? Sorry you left us, huh?"

"Not when I buy a new car," Walgreen said and added softly, "I'm in trouble."

"Yeah. We know."

"How?"

"We keep track of our old people. We do guard the President, you know, and we like to know what our old friends do all the time."

"I didn't think it was still that tight."

"Since Kennedy, it stays that tight."

"That was a helluva shot that guy got from the window," Walgreen said. "Nobody can stop that kind of stuff."

"You know better than I do. When you're bodyguard to the President, nobody measures your success by how many assassination attempts fail."

"How much do you know about me?"

"We know you think you're in trouble. We know that if you stayed with us, you would have gone to the top. We know some local police are making noises and moves on your behalf that

9

you're supposed to be unaware of. How good are your locals, Ernie?"

"Locals," said Walgreen.

"Oh," said the district man. It was a gray-furnitured office with the antiseptic cubicity of those who have very specific jobs and need not be expansive to the public. Walgreen sat down. It was not the kind of office that even old friends offered each other a drink in. It was more a file cabinet drawer than an office as Walgreen knew it, and he was very glad he had left the Secret Service for carpets and drinks and golf dates and all the cozy amenities of American business.

"I'm in trouble, but I can't dot the 'i' on it. It was just a phone call, but the voice . . . it was the voice. I don't know how much you know about business, but there are people you know who are just for real. It's a calmness in their voices, a precision. I don't know. This one had it."

"Ernie, I respect you. You know that."

"What are you driving at?" asked Walgreen.

"A phone call isn't enough."

"What do I have to do to get you guys in on it? Be killed?"

"All right. Why does this person want to kill you?"

"I don't know. He just said I should get all the protection I could."

"Were you drinking?"

"No, I was not drinking. I was working."

"Ernie, that's a standard crank call you got. That's a standard. They tell you to get a gun, to put on extra men, 'because, buddy, I'm gonna blow your brains out.' Ernie. Please."

"It was for real. I know standard crank calls. You're lucky you've got computers nowadays to keep track of them. I know crank calls. Moreover, I think you know I can tell the difference. This voice was not a crank. I don't know the why of it but, between you and me, this one's for real."

"You know I'm helpless, Ernie."

"Why?"

"Because in a report, it doesn't have Ernie Walgreen looking me in the eye like you're looking now and me knowing, right where you know it, that these people are for real. Knowing it in the gut."

"Got any suggestions? I've had a lot of practice making money."

"Use it, Ernie."

"With whom?"

"After Kennedy got shot out from underneath us, there was a big shakeup here. Pretty quiet but pretty big."

"I know. I had something to do with it," Walgreen said. The district man looked at him with mild surprise.

"Anyway," the district man said, "it didn't do anything because there was no way we could have stopped a guy getting in a shot like Oswald did, but we had to look like we made some changes so we could tell Johnson that the Secret Service that lost Kennedy isn't the same as the one guarding you now. In the shakeup, some good men, really good men, quit. They were very bitter. And I can't blame them. They have their own security agency now . . ."

"I don't need some retired policeman in a blue uniform to discourage shoplifting."

"No, they're not your normal corporate security. They do super stuff for super people and I'm talking about protecting foreign heads of state too, designing their palaces and everything. They're even better on protection than we are because their clients don't have to go running around to every airport crowd shaking hands. God, that terrifies me. Why couldn't a Howard Hughes hermit be President instead of some damned politician? It's always a politician." He paused. "What'd you mean, you had something to do with the shakeup?" he asked.

Walgreen shrugged. "I did some work for the President," he said, "in the security area."

"Which President?"

"All of them. Until this one."

The firm name of retired Secret Service people was *Paldor*. He said the Secret Service had sent him and he was ushered into the kind of offices he was used to, a touch of strong elegance with a good view.

Cherry blossoms and the Potomac. A friendly Scotch on the rocks. A sympathetic ear. The man's name was Lester Pruel and Walgreen knew something about him. He was six feet one, tanned and healthy, with sharp, discerning blue eyes. He had a comfortable smoothness about him that government employees, in contrast, seemed to lack, the sort of manner that indicated he made decisions. The decision he made for Ernest Walgreen was 'no.'

"I'd like to help you," said Pruel. His gray-blond hair was marcelled in a very dry look. "And we do go out of our way for old friends from the Service. But fella, it's one frigging phone call."

"I've got money."

"We charge a hundred thousand for just a

look. Now that's for sending some people out to figure out what we'd really charge you when we get down to work. We're not sending a bunch of cadoodles in blue uniforms and tin badges, two steps off the welfare rolls. This is real security."

"That's a lot of money."

"Fella, we'd do it for nothing, if we thought it was real. We like our contacts with our kind of people. We'd even like you, Walgreen, to come to work for us. Except you look like you're doing pretty well for an old service man."

"I'm going to die," said Walgreen.

"Have you been sort of light on sex lately? I mean, sometimes at your age we lose a sense of proportion about things. Now both you and I know from training that one phone call . . ."

The next night, Ernest Walgreen of Minneapolis, Minnesota, was flying to Manchester Airport in New Hampshire to identify the body of his wife.

A syringe had been pressed thoroughly into her temple, as if somebody had attempted to inject something into her brain. Except this was a veterinarian's syringe and it had been empty. What had been injected into the brain was the large needle to make the brain stop working.

And, as an added measure, a good dose of air. Air in the bloodstream killed. The body was found in the back seat of her brother's car, with no telltale fingerprints on the car, none on the syringe. It was as if someone or something had come into this little northern community, done its job, and left. There was no known motive.

The casket with her body was already at the Manchester Airport when Walgreen arrived. Lester Pruel was standing next to the casket. His face was grim.

"We're all sorry. We didn't know. We'll give you everything. Again. I'm sorry, I'm sorry. We thought, well, it was just a phone call. On the face of it, you've got to admit . . . look, we can't bring her back but we can keep you alive. If you want us to."

"Yes, I do," said Ernest Walgreen. Mildred would have wanted that, he thought. She loved life. Death was no excuse for the living to give up on it.

She was buried at Arcadian Angels cemetery, outside Olivia, county seat of Renville, amid the rich farmlands where Walgreen's father had been born and where his own son now plowed with tractor the ground that Walgreen had once plowed with horses.

It was the strangest funeral Olivia, Minnesota, had ever seen. Well-dressed men stopped mourners coming to the graveside to ask them what the metal object was in their pockets. They would not let them go near the grave unless they first showed what the metal was. An Olivia businessman, an old friend of the Walgreen family, said the strangers must have devices somewhere like airports had that detected metal on people.

A nearby hilltop was scoured and a hunter was told to move on. When he refused his gun was taken. He said he was going to the police. The men told him, "Fine, but after the funeral."

The car Ernest Walgreen drove up in was also strange. While other tires left the pattern of their rubber-gripping tread in the fresh spring earth, these dug in a good four inches. The car was a heavy one. A youngster who got through the men

14

always surrounding the limousine said the metal "didn't make no hollow sound, like usual."

It wasn't a car. It was a tank with wheels designed to look like a car. And there were guns. Hidden under suitcases, behind newspapers, inside hats, but guns to be sure.

Residents wondered whether Ernest Walgreen had gone into crime.

"The Mafia," they whispered. But someone pointed out that the men didn't look like Mafia types.

"Shoot," said someone else in a rare bit of wisdom, "the Mafia's probably as American as you and me."

Someone else remembered that Ernest Walgreen had once worked for the government. At least that was the rumor.

"It's easy. Ernie must have become a spy for the CIA. He must be one of those fellas what has to be protected 'cause he shot up so many of them Russians."

Walgreen watched Mildred's white ash coffin being lowered into the narrow hole and thought, as he always did at funerals, how narrow the holes were and how small the last space was. And thinking of Mildred going down into that hole, he broke. There was nothing left but tears. And he had to tell himself it was not his wife disappearing, but the body. She had gone when the life went out of her. And he remembered her one last time, fumbling with her purse at the airport, and he thought: *All right, let them end it now. Whoever it is. Let them finish me now.*

So deep was his grief, it demolished hate and any desire for revenge.

The Paldor security team decided his home was too exposed to risk. Too many blind entrances and exits.

"It's an assassin's delight," said Pruel, who had personally taken over Walgreen's protection.

For Walgreen, it was a relief to leave that house because Mildred was still there, in every part of it, from her potter's wheel to the mirror she had cracked.

"I have a vacation cabin in Sun Valley," said Walgreen. "But I need something to do. I don't want to think. It hurts too much."

"We'll have plenty of work for you," said Pruel.

The Sun Valley house proved to be an ideal fort, with what Pruel called a few modifications. Paldor refused to take any payment. To keep Walgreen's mind occupied, Les Pruel explained the latest techniques in top security.

"For all history, you've had imposing stone forts and moats and men standing around with weapons. That is until a new technique came about. Maybe it was stumbled on, I don't know, but it changed everything. And what it was is sort of magic."

"Mystery."

"No, no. Magic like Houdini. Like magicians. Illusion. In other words what you do is present something that isn't there. It sounds risky but it's the safest damned thing that ever was. It's absolutely one hundred percent foolproof. If Kennedy had it, he never would have been assassinated in Dallas. Never. Oswald wouldn't have known where to shoot."

Walgreen followed every step and as each new

device was installed, he realized the genius of the new technique of illusion. It was not to stop an assassin from trying. Rather you wanted him to try because that was the greatest trap.

First the windows in the house that appeared to be normal see-through glass were changed so that what you saw inside was really three or four feet off. You really saw reflections from the polarized glass.

And there were two access roads that were opened wide. Or so it seemed. But the roads were wired and if cars didn't stop when ordered to by someone who appeared to be a forest ranger but was really a Paldor agent, the road would suddenly open up at a specified point, leaving two ditches in front and in back of any car which refused to stop.

The slope of the hill housed another electrical system that picked up urine odors of any human body. It had been developed in Vietnam. And all the surrounding hills were cabined by people who appeared to be just vacationers when in reality they were Paldor agents.

The illusion was that Ernest Walgreen's country cabin was a country cabin, instead of an electronic trap. It worked on the assassin's mind so that when he saw Walgreen puttering around in his garden from a nearby hill, he would think: *I can kill that man just by driving up and putting a bullet in him. I can kill that man anytime I want. And I'd better do it now because he'll never be so open again.*

Now if some assassin had a rifle on that nearby hill, a woman fixing her fence would tap an electronic signal and the assassin would not only fail to get off a shot but would in all likelihood end up with a bullet himself.

There was no way, Walgreen realized, that anyone could reach him and he was sorry he had not had this earlier so Mildred could share this safety with him. The pine cabin was protected from every angle of approach. And on August fifth, as the heat crossed the great American plains backing the midwest, the foundation of the cabin rose. And when the temperature hit 92 degrees, a very volatile explosive, waiting in the foundation since spring, spread the house in one very loud bang across the Sun Valley recreation area.

Along with its sole occupant, Ernest Walgreen.

In Washington, this matter was called to the attention of the President of the United States. An Annapolis graduate and a physicist, he was not about to be panicked.

"Murder seems like a local crime," he said.

"It's not just murder, sir," said his aide in a thick Southern drawl, so syrupy most Northerners drummed their fingers waiting for the man to get through the vowels and on to those rare consonants Southerners occasionally allowed to enter their speech.

"What is it then?" asked the President.

"It was an assassination that might be a warning for us. We believe it is."

"Then give it to the Secret Service. They're responsible for my protection. I'm fairly certain this man didn't have as good protection as I do and besides, assassination is always with a President of this country. It's part of the job."

"Well, sir, this isn't just any old assassination.

You see, sir, it wasn't that he had worse protection that you. The Secret Service tells us he had better. And the people who killed him . . . well, they say you're next, sir."

CHAPTER TWO

His name was Remo and he was exercising. Not the way a high school coach would exercise a team did this man exercise. He did not push muscles or strain ligaments or drive his wind to the breaking point so that the breaking point would be farther back next time. Straining and pushing were things long past, only dim remembrances of how other men used their bodies incorrectly.

Nothing fighting itself ever worked to its utmost. But that which did what was attuned to itself was the most effective it could be. A blade of grass growing and reaching for light could crack concrete. A mother, not reminding herself she was a woman and therefore incapable of strength, could—to save her baby—lift the rear end of an automobile off the ground. Water falling with gravity cut through rock.

To be most powerfully human required divesting oneself of that which was most human, a pure undiluted thought. And Remo was one with himself as he moved out smoothly and his body, with the snap of his toes extended out and restful with the gravity, let the forty-five feet of air between him and the sidewalk below take him down from the building ledge.

There were forces that acted on the body in free-falling flight, that if one allowed fear-triggered adrenalin to dominate, could crush the bones of the body as it collided with the pavement.

What one had to do was to be able to coordinate the meeting with the pavement . . . to make the fall slower at the bottom.

It would not be really slower, any more than baseballs pitched to the great hitter Ted Williams were slower than those pitched to anyone else. But Ted Williams could see the stitches on the pitched baseballs and therefore could hit the ball with his bat more easily.

Remo, whose last name had also been Williams a long time ago but was no relation to the ballplayer, also slowed things down by becoming faster with his mind, the most powerful human organ but the one used least by most people. Less than eight percent of the human brain was ever used. It had become almost a vestigial organ.

If men ever learned to use that mind, they would, like Remo—his hands extended now before him—catch the world on the sidewalk, compress it back up so that there was no sudden push on the body, but only a minutely accurate division of stress, until . . . no more. No stress and back up on feet and look around. Salamander Street, Los Angeles. Empty sidewalk, just daybreak in Watts.

Remo picked up the two twenty-five cent pieces that had fallen out of his pocket and looked around for more change. Early morning was always quiet in black neighborhoods, a special nothing-doing time of day, where if you wanted you could do compression dives off buildings and no one would go running around saying:

"Hey, did you see that guy do that? Did you see what I saw?"

Remo was six feet tall with high cheekbones and dark eyes that had an electric cool about them. He was thin and only his extraordinarily thick wrists might indicate that here was something other than the normal decaying flesh most men allow their bodies to become.

There had been high dives by people without full body control, but they used foam and inflated giant pillows to absorb the smack crack of forty-eight feet so that the material, not the diver, controlled the impact.

They also lacked control of their organs, assuming the intestines and liver acted like independent planets. Considering what foulness they consumed for energy and how they breathed, they were fortunate that cells were allowed to control themselves. If the people had done it, they would hardly have lived to reach puberty.

Remo looked back at the building.

Exercise now had become a re-realization of what his body was and what he did and thought and breathed. The flat slap of a soft rubber tire hobbled through a pothole two blocks down. A yellow car with a light on top indicating a cab for hire slowly came up the street.

Remo waved at him. He had to get back to the hotel. He could run it but he did not need the running, and if he should be fortunate enough to luck into a cab at this hour and this place, why not?

Remo waited as the cab came close. There were important things to do that morning. Upstairs

22

had come up with a new wrinkle. Remo could never follow the code words and always ended up snarling at middle-aged Dr. Harold W. Smith:

"If you can say it, say it. If not, don't. I'm not going to piddle around with letters and numbers and dates. If you want to play with yourself, feel free. But this code nickypoo is the pits."

Smith, who to the outside world ran a sanitarium called Folcroft on Long Island Sound, was in the west to deliver personally something he had been unable to say in code on the telephone. The few words Remo had understood meant that it had to do with the new President and some safety measure. Smith was to be at the hotel for exactly ten minutes and out again, under the rather workable and usually successful theory that if there is something that is dangerous, one should do it as quickly as possible. Don't give disaster a lot of operating time.

And there was always a danger in Smith meeting Remo, because to be seen with the killer arm of CURE would be a crucial link to admitting that there even was a CURE, the government's extra-legal organization, set up in a desperate attempt to stave off the impending chaos of a government weakened by its own laws but still resolved to administer them publicly.

Remo watched the cab slow down, then take off by him. The driver had seen him. Remo knew that. The driver had looked right at him, slowed, then stepped on the gas.

So Remo kicked off the loose loafers, so that the soles of his feet could skim better along the pavement.

He wore a tight black tee shirt over loose gray pants that snapped as the wind pressure whipped on the skimming, darting legs. He was moving on the cab, out into the cool morning asphalt of the gutter. Stench-burning smell of slum and slam. Bang onto the rear of the cab. Remo heard all four doors lock.

Cabs had become little fortresses nowadays because sticking a gun in the back of the head of a driver had become a very easy way to collect money. So the American taxi in large cities had evolved into a rolling bunker, with bulletproof windshields behind the driver's head and doors that locked simultaneously with a switch near the driver's radio and a special beep in his dispatcher to indicate that a robbery was in progress. This driver did not have a chance to use the beeper.

The unfortified weakness of the cab was the top. Remo felt it as his body pressed against it. He crushed his straightened fingers down into the thin metal sheet of roofing and, closing his hand on vinyl interior upholstery compressed with insulation between and bright yellow painted metal on top, and he yanked, ripping off a slab of the roof like someone separating Swiss cheese slices. One, two, three rips and he could wedge himself down next to the driver who, by now, was accelerating, twisting, slamming on brakes, and screaming all sorts of incipient mayhem to his dispatchers.

"Mind if I ride in the front?" asked Remo.

"No. Go right ahead. Want a cigarette?" said the driver. He laughed lightly. He wet his pants. The wet went down his leg to the accelerator. Every once in a while, he looked up over him where the roof had suddenly opened to great metal-chomping rips. He had thought he was being attacked by a dinosaur that ate metal. The thin man with the thick wrists told him where he wanted to go. It was a hotel.

"You really know how to hail a cab, fella," the driver said.

"You didn't stop," said Remo.

"I'll stop next time. I got nothin' against anybody but you stop in the colored neighborhoods and it's your life."

"What color?" Remo asked.

"Whaddya mean, what color? Black color. You think I'm talkin' orange already? Colored colored."

"There's yellow, there's red, there's brown, there's pale white. There's off white, there's pink. Sometimes," Remo said, "there's even a burnt umber perambulating around."

"Spook," said the driver.

But Remo was contemplating the rainbow of people. The divisions by simple color of black and white or red and yellow were not really the colors of people but racial designations. Yet races were not the big difference. The big difference was how people used themselves, raised themselves closer to what they could be. There were undoubtedly differences between groups but they were inordinately small compared to the difference between what all people were and what all people could be.

It was like a car. One car might have eight cylinders and another six and another four. If none of the cars used more than one cylinder, then there was no real difference among them. Such it was with man. Any man who used two of his cylinders was considered a great athlete.

And of course, there were one or two who used all eight cylinders.

"Forty-two Zebra, you still being eaten?"

"No. Nothing is wrong," said the driver.

"Is that your code for trouble?" Remo asked. "That nothing is wrong?"

"Nah," said the driver.

"That is inordinately silly," Remo said. "Here I am sitting in the front seat with you and that police car several blocks back there is going to chase us. Now if there's a fight, look who's right in the middle."

"What police car?"

"Back there."

"Oh, Jesus," said the driver, finally seeing police markings back down the broad street.

Up ahead, another police cruiser stuck its nose out into the street.

"I guess we'd better stop and give ourselves up," said the driver.

"Let's run for it," Remo said. He winked at the driver who felt the wheel move on its own accord, and then that lunatic, the guy who had ripped the roof and climbed in the torn hole, that guy who didn't know how to get into a cab decently, was leaning into him. He was steering. Then the cab was going crazy, throating out full throttle, whip, zip, almost hitting the squad car that was in front. Now it was in back, pursuing the cab, then up onto the sidewalk and taking a phalanx of morning garbage cans like bowling pins.

The cabdriver glanced into the rearview mirror. Strike. There wasn't a garbage can left standing.

Sirens screamed. Tires squealed. The driver moaned. He couldn't even budge the wheel from the lunatic. He tried punching. He had been middleweight champion of his high school, so he punched. Right and left and the lunatic had his hands on the wheel and was leaning into him and he missed. The lunatic was anchored to the wheel. But both punches missed. Right and left missed.

How did the lunatic move his body that way? It was as if the lunatic could move his chest, attached to two arms attached to the steering wheel, faster than the driver could throw punches. Right and left punches. Punches from the former middleweight champion of Pacifica High.

Guy was good. Great maybe. Rips out car roofs with his hands. Wasn't that good a roof, maybe. Lunatic could dodge punches while going eighty-five miles an hour. Eighty-five miles an hour?

The driver moaned. They were going to be killed. At eighty-five miles an hour, you weren't driving in Los Angeles, you were aiming.

The driver tried to kick the lunatic's foot off the pedal. It didn't kick. The lunatic could hold his foot out with more stability than the car itself. It was like kicking a lamp post.

"I'll sit back and enjoy it," said the driver. Lunatics, he knew, had abnormal strength.

"Your cab insured?"

"Insurance never covers," said the driver.

"Sometimes it covers more," said Remo. "I know a lawyer."

"Look. You want to do me a favor? Leave me alone."

"All right. Bye," said Remo and kicked open the door to his right and let the cab careen across an empty lot as he floated free and out, the sidewalk moving quickly beneath him, his legs running—which was the key, to keep on moving quickly and not to stop—out onto the street, behind the hotel and in through the alley.

He entered through a back kitchen, asking who bought the fresh meat for the hotel. Workers didn't notice salesmen coming into a kitchen area, looking to sell something. For a guest to enter, however, would have attracted attention. The kitchen reeked of eggs bubbling in cow grease called butter.

At Remo's suite of rooms, a shaken Smith waited at the door, face gaunt, hands knuckle-white over his briefcase, his middle-aged body taut with anger.

"What in God's name was that downstairs?"

"What downstairs?"

"The police. The chase. I saw from the window. The taxicab you came flying out of."

"You wanted me to be on time, didn't you? You said this was important enough for you to come out here personally. That's how important it was. You said you could only stay ten minutes for the meeting, so that there would be no chance of us being seen together. You said this was touchy. What's touchy?"

"Presidential assassination," said Smith. He took a step toward the door.

Remo stopped him.

"So?"

"I can't be seen here with you. Not even in the same hotel. With the lunatic assassination theories and committees running around, they could easily turn over a rock and find all of us."

"What's the problem, other than you've lost your sense of reason?"

"The problem is the President of the United States is going to be assassinated. I don't have time to go into how I am sure of it, but you know we have our sources and our calculations."

28

Remo knew. He knew that the organization, for well over a decade now, had been secretly prompting law enforcement agencies to do their jobs properly, leaking information to the press on great frauds and, as a last resort, unleashing Remo himself during a crisis. He also knew that since the advent of the organization, the chaos had grown in the country. The streets were not safe; the police were no better. There was even a very well-paid police commissioner on a national television show complaining how the police were only "a very efficient army of occupation for the poor."

The one thing that man's police was not was "very efficient." Pregnant women were shoved alive into incinerators in that man's city. His own police rioted. Never before had so many people paid so much money for so little protection.

Remo had become hardened over the years but that was too hard to swallow. There had been a war against crime and chaos and the first to surrender had been the police. It was as if an army had not only let an invader through, they had demanded from their helpless country a higher tribute for their worthlessness. Then again, maybe the citizens had abandoned the decent policemen first. Whatever it was, the civilization was slipping.

So another politician's life did not send shivers of respect through Remo as it did through Dr. Harold W. Smith.

"So the President's going to be killed. So what?" Remo said.

"Have you seen the Vice President?" Smith said.

"We've got to save the President," Remo said.

"We have to, but not for that reason. This country is so weak we can't afford to lose another President. We're trying to convince the President that his life is in danger and he may need added protection. But he says it's up to God, Remo. Remo, we just can't take another assassination. I can't stay. You brought the police here. When I saw them, I gave Chiun the details. I don't know how you two slip in and out of dragnets and things so easily, but for me this is a dangerous place. Convince the President he's in danger. Goodbye."

Remo let Smith leave, his body sweating the heavy meat odors, his face persimmonously acid. A lemon bitter pall coated his whole demeanor.

Smith also left Remo with an awesome problem. For Smith, a westerner, did not understand what words meant when he spoke to Chiun, a Master of Sinanju, the age-old house that had provided assassins throughout history.

Remo knew he was in trouble when he saw the delighted smile on the face of Chiun, a delicate uprising half moon on a yellow parchment face, wisps of white beard and hair like a touch of silver cotton candy. He stood in a regal pose, his gold and crimson kimono made by ancient hands, flowing with the grace of an emperor's gown.

"At last, a proper use of a Master of Sinanju," said Chiun, his eighty-year-old voice as high as dry brakes in a desert. "Lo, these many years we have been degraded by working against the criminals and all manner of lowlife in your country but now, in his wisdom, your Emperor Smith has come to his senses."

"Jesus, no," said Remo. "Don't tell me." The large lacquered steamer trunks were already

30

packed in Chiun's room, sealed with wax, lest any be opened without Chiun's knowledge.

"First, Smith was wise enough to at last put the true master in charge," Chiun said.

"You're not in charge, Little Father," said Remo.

"No back talk," said Chiun. "You are not even standing in a respectful bow."

"C'mon, get off it. What did Smith really say?"

"He said, looking out at that disgusting, disgraceful scene in the street, how you, while learning the greatness of Sinanju in one respect, had become insane in the other."

"And what did you say?"

"I said we had done wonders considering we had a white man to work with."

"And what did he say?"

"He said he felt sorry for someone as kind and understanding as your teacher who had endured your shoddiness of breathing and blood control."

"He did not say that."

"Your breathing has gotten so irregular even a white meat-eater can hear the crude rasps."

"I've corrected that and the only thing someone like Smitty knows about breathing is that it's bad when it stops forever. He knows no more about breathing than you do about computers."

"I know computers have to be plugged into sockets. I know that," said Chiun. "I know when I hear slander from an ingrate against the very House that found him as dirt and through labor and discipline and with the expenditure of awesome knowledge, transformed a sluggish half-dead body into a large part of what he could be."

"Little Father," said Remo to the man who had indeed transformed him, although in often very

31

annoying ways, "Smith could not possibly understand anything about breathing, any more than you could understand anything about the democratic process."

"I know you lie to yourself a lot. You tell yourself you have friends you choose but you really have emperors like everyone else."

"What did Smitty say?"

"He said your breathing was a disgrace."

"What were the specific words?"

"He heard the noise and looked out the window and said, 'what a disgrace.'"

"That was 'cause the cops were following me. And he didn't want commotion. He wasn't talking about my breathing."

"Do not be a fool," Chiun said. "You lumbered out of that vehicle, breathing like a stuck hippo, as if you had to concentrate to keep your nostrils open. Smith sees this and then you think that he is concerned not about your breathing but about the police who are no danger to anyone, especially someone who will give them coins?"

"Yes. Especially since I worked out that breathing thing."

"You went high?" Chiun asked.

"How else?"

"I thought you looked almost adequate down there," said Chiun. And then with a modicum of joy, he outlined the instructions that Smith had hurriedly given to him.

He and Remo would enter the presidential palace.

"The White House," Remo said.

"Correct," said Chiun. "Emperor Smith wants us to let this other man who thinks he is the em-

32

peror know where the real power is. That he who has Sinanju as his sword is emperor in any land, and that any man may call himself emperor but only one is. That is what Smith wants."

"I don't understand," Remo said.

"We call it the leaf. It is an old thing but I let Emperor Smith think he had thought of it, although for generations the House has done this thing hundreds of times. It is quite common."

"What is 'the leaf'?" Remo asked. "I never heard of it before."

"When you look at a forest in the springtime from a distance, you see green. And you say the green is the forest because that is what you see. But this is not true. And when you get closer you see the green is made up of leaves and you say, aha, the leaves are the forest. But this is not true. You must be really close before you realize that the leaves are but little things made by trees and that the trees are the real forest.

"Thus, the real power in a land is often not he whom the people think is emperor, but someone far wiser, such as he who has grasped the House of Sinanju to his heart.

"And then it is the duty of the real emperor's assassin to show the false emperor who the real emperor is, show the leaf that it is only a part of the tree. It is a common thing. We have done it many times."

And by the "we" Chiun meant the House of Sinanju, the Masters who had rented themselves out to kings and pharaohs and emperors throughout the ages to support the poor village of Sinanju on the coast of the West Korea Bay. Years before, Chiun, the last Master, had taken the job of training Remo, and every year the secret organization CURE sent tribute to Chiun's North Korean village.

"And we are supposed to do what specifically?" Remo asked.

"Put fear into the President's heart. Expose his vulnerability. Make him cower and plead for the mercy of Emperor Smith. It is good to be working among proper folk again."

"You must have gotten something wrong, Little Father," said Remo. "I don't think Smith wants that done to the President."

"Perhaps," Chiun said, "we will take the President at night and bring him to a pit of hyenas and hold him over it until he swears eternal loyalty to Smith."

"I'm pretty sure that's not what Smith wants. You see, Smith serves the country; he doesn't rule it."

"They all say that but they really want to rule. Perhaps, instead of the hyenas, we can cripple the President's finest general. Who is America's finest general?"

"We don't have fine generals anymore, Little Father. We have accountants who know how to spend money."

"Who is the most fearsome fighter in the land?"

"We don't have any."

"No matter. It is time that America saw what a true assassin is like instead of all the amateurs that have plagued this land."

"Little Father, I am sure Smitty doesn't want the President harmed," Remo said.

"Quiet. I am in charge now. I am not just a

teacher anymore. Perhaps we can remove the President's ears as a lesson."

"Little Father, let me explain a few things. Hopefully," Remo said. With little hope.

CHAPTER THREE

The President was hearing from some "good ole boys" how "this here White House, it got more protection than a twenty-year-old coonhound with bad breath and a kerosene ass."

"My advisers tell me I don't have enough protection," said the President softly. He worked at a table stacked with reports. He could read as fast as some men could think and liked to work four uninterrupted hours at a stretch. During those times he could ingest a week's information and still there would be more. He had discovered early in his presidency that a man without priorities in that office was a man who swamped helpless immediately. You and your staff culled what you absolutely had to do and then added what you should do and then cut that in half to make a work week only two weeks' full.

In that manner did men age in this office. No one ever left the presidency of the United States young.

"Y'all gotta remember, sir, these boys up heah in Washington, they sure 'nough know how to worry."

"They say I'm a dead man unless I listen to them. They say we've had serious threats."

"Shoot. These boys'll sell you the smoke from a horse's nostrils. Everybody heah looking to protect you from something. For a lot of money."

"You don't think I'm in danger? A man was killed in Sun Valley, just as an example to me, they said."

"Sure you in danger, sir. Everybody's always in danger."

"I've told the Secret Service people who guard me that I think I've got enough protection and I don't want to be bothered anymore. There are other things more pressing. But I wonder sometimes. It's not just my life. This country can't take another presidential assassination. The air is already so poisoned with rumors and doubts and stories about conspiracies and plots and counterplots."

"To say nothin' of us losing our first President since James K. Polk. There was a long while there we didn't have nobody from the South. Long while. Don' worry. We ain' gonna lose you."

The President smiled graciously. His old friend from back home who had been a state trooper showed him what his own Secret Service had shown him, how the White House itself was impregnable and that the only time anyone ever really got through the gates was when the President was on a trip somewhere.

"You already got the best heah. Cain't do no better, sir," said the old friend from Georgia. "Why, cain't even get a gnat through these people. They got guards guarding guards guarding guards and more radar and stuff like that than any place on earth."

37

"I don't know," said the President. He knew without saying that too many people had come too close to too many Presidents recently. Lunatics had gotten a loaded revolver to within a handshake of the previous President. Someone had even gotten off a shot. A man had crashed a truck through the White House gate just the year before and a woman with a stick of dynamite on her body had been apprehended within the White House.

They were psychotics, the Secret Service told him. The could never do more than get close. And professionals wouldn't even get as far as those psychotics who were willing to risk their lives.

Perhaps, the President had said.

But the old friend from Georgia saw something a cabinet member might miss. It was that slight nod of the head while appearing to agree.

"You got somethin' up your sleeve, don't you?" said the friend.

"Maybe. Let's say I hope. I can't tell you."

"Well, if it's a defense secret, you don't have to. I been using up your time too much already. Like the ninth puppy on an eight-tit bitch."

"No. I'm glad you came. I'm glad for these moments. A man gets to think of himself as too big and too important when he doesn't keep in touch with people who knew him before the rest of the world did."

"Good luck on your ace in the hole," said the friend, a big half-moon grin from ear to ear. They shook hands goodbye.

"I'm not a gambler," said the President. He worked two more hours, until fifteen minutes before midnight, then went to the private rooms of what was, in effect, America's presidential palace. He could not forget what his friend had said, that even the guards had guards, but also he could not shake that clinging, gnawing hunch that the leader of the most powerful nation on earth might be vulnerable. To anyone.

His wife was asleep as he entered the bedroom. Quietly he went to the bureau by the immense bathroom. In the bottom drawer was the red telephone that he had used only once before.

It was not an instrument to his liking because he knew that for more than twenty years now, American Presidents had allowed and relied on an illegal organization, one that was supposed to do its job and disappear when the nation was through its crisis. And now the organization, and the crisis, seemed permanent. He did not order it to shut down when he discovered that much of the uncovered criminal activity would have grown completely out of bounds if it had not been for the secret organization CURE. At least twice it had saved the nation.

But it was as illegal as hell.

The President carried the red phone by its long cord into the bathroom and lifted the receiver. The telephone had no dial.

"Yes," came the voice. It was Dr. Harold W. Smith.

"Are you going to do that demonstration?"

"Yes."

"When?"

"Should be tonight. A day to get where you are and then ten minutes to get through whatever you've got in the way of protection," Smith said.

"Ten minutes?" the President said disbelievingly.

"If they walk."

"Don't they have to reconnoiter? Figure out a plan?"

"No, sir. You see, the Oriental is a teacher and his House has been doing this for quite a few centuries. The Secret Service might think they have something new, but the Oriental and the white man have handled things like that before, and the Oriental's ancestors for thousands of years. Their skill is their memory."

"What about electronics? Electronics haven't been around for centuries," the President said.

"They don't seem to have any trouble," said Smith.

"Just walk through? All the guards. All the surveillance. I can't believe it."

The President cradled the red receiver between his sweater shoulder and cheek. He held the base in front of him like a young girl gripping a communion bouquet. He always rolled his eyes back up into his head when he spoke privately. The receiver handle suddenly slipped from his cheek as if it were a tooth yanked from a novocaine-numbed jaw. The President felt the yank as the receiver slipped away. His head jerked. His cheek touched his shoulder. Assuming the receiver had fallen, he instinctively reached for it. He felt warm flesh. The flesh pushed his hand back as if he were meeting a wall.

There was a man wearing a dark tee shirt, gray slacks, and loafers standing in the presidential bathroom with the President's red telephone. And talking into it.

"Hey, Smitty. We have some confusion here. Yeah. Everything is fouled up as usual. Excuse me, Mr. President, business."

"Should I wait outside?" the President asked drily.

"No, you can stay. It's your business. Yeah, Smitty, he's standing right here. What do you want with him anyway? He's all right. He just looks a little dazed. Well, Chiun says you want this guy's face stuffed in it or something. Oh, oh. All right. Here. He wants to talk to you."

The President took the telephone. "Yes," he said. "No," he said. "My god, I didn't even hear him. It was like he came from nowhere. My god. I never knew there were people who could . . . yes, of course, Dr. Smith. Thank you all." He put his hand over the receiver and spoke to the intruder:

"Is there a Mr. Chiun outside there?"

"Hey, Little Father," Remo said. "It's Smitty. For you." Remo took the phone. The President saw a long-fingernailed hand reach into the bathroom, a golden kimono sleeve dropping from it like water over a cliff. The hand was parchment yellow. The fingernails were the longest he had ever seen on a person.

The phone disappeared outside the door.

"Yes, glorious emperor Smith. According to thy will. Forever and eternal. Rule in the glory of thy throne." The voice was squeaky. Then came the angry jabbering of an Oriental language as the phone was returned to the hook.

An aged Oriental followed the arm and telephone into the bathroom. He was smaller than the President's twelve-year-old daughter and undoubtedly lighter. He was angry. The wisps of beard trembled. He jabbered at Remo for what must have been three minutes.

"What did he say?" asked the President.

41

"Who? Smitty or Chiun?"

"This must be Chiun then. How do you do, Mr. Chiun."

The Master of Sinanju looked at the President of the most powerful nation in the world. He saw the hand stretched out in friendship, he saw the smile on the man's face. He turned away, folding his hands into his kimono.

"Did I say something?" asked the President.

"No," said Remo. "He's mad about something."

"Does he know that I am President of the United States?"

"Oh yeah, he knows that. He's just disappointed, is all."

"Over what?"

"Never mind. You wouldn't understand. It's his way of thinking and I don't think you'd grasp it."

"Try me," said the President, more ordering than requesting.

"You wouldn't understand."

"I am conversant with the Japanese."

"Oh, my god," said Remo. "Don't call him Japanese. He's Korean. Would you want to be called French?"

"That depends on where I am."

"Or German? Or English? You're American. Well, he's Korean."

"The best kind," said Chiun with cold hauteur. "From the nicest part and the nicest village in the nicest part. Sinanju, glory of the world, center of the earth, upon which all planets look for reverence."

"Sinanju? Sinanju?" asked the President. He had worked on submarines in his Navy days, and in the submarine service the small village on the west Korean bay had been discussed. American submarines had been going there for some reason for the last twenty years. Stories about delivering gold to a spy system or something, but every submariner had heard the tales of how every year one American submarine had to make the trip into enemy waters.

"Glory to that name," said Chiun.

"Oh, of course. Glory to it. Somehow that and submarines seem to be connected."

"Tribute," said Remo. "America pays tribute to Sinanju."

"For what?" asked the President.

"For him to train me," Remo said.

"In what?"

"Well ... things," Remo said. And the President heard the Oriental emit another stream of invective in Korean.

"What did he say?" the President asked.

"He said all the training was never really well used. It's what he's mad about."

"What?"

"Well, Sinanju is the great House of assassins. They sort of rented themselves out to kings and the like through the ages."

Chiun poked a long fingernail into the space between Remo and the President.

"So that children will not have to drown in the cold waters with empty bellies. We save children," said Chiun angrily.

Remo shrugged toward the President. "He means that, oh, maybe twenty-eight hundred years ago, way before Christ, the village had to get rid of its babies because they couldn't afford to feed them. It was a poor village."

43

"Because of the soil," said Chiun. "Because of the degenerates who ruled. Because of foreign armies."

"Anyway," Remo said, "until the Masters of Sinanju began renting themselves out around the world for tribute, the village starved. They saved the village from starving, but they like to say they are saving the babies from death."

"There are a lot of Masters?" asked the President.

"No. There's Chiun now, and there's me. But we are all part of the tradition of Sinanju so that when we talk about the Masters, it's as if they're all alive. You think of time as line and you're in the middle and the past is behind you on the line and the future is ahead of you. But we look at the time like a big plate, so anytime is just another part of the round plate."

"And they are teachers?" the President asked.

"No. Chiun is the first who has taught an outsider."

"Well, what do they do?"

"The House of Sinanju is assassins," said Remo.

"He was mad because he was told not to kill me, right?" the President said.

"Well, actually, yes. You see, you're the first President he's ever had and we haven't been doing any heads of state. It's like if you were President of the United States and then suddenly you get hired to be President of a grocery store. It's a step down, see? You don't see."

"He was going to kill me," said the President. His face blanched.

"I told you you wouldn't understand," said Remo.

"I understand my life is in danger. Who let you in?"

"There's no 'let' involved," Remo said.

"Your incompetence," said Chiun.

"Hey, Prez. Let me show you how open everything is around here. You're dead meat. I mean, you're a bun on a plate. We could pepper you like scrambled eggs." Remo smiled. "Protection? You don't have any. Come on, Smitty says we're supposed to save your duff. We'll show you."

In later days, the President would ask questions of doctors, of top CIA brass, trying to learn if certain things could be illusions.

"Let's say, for example," the President would say, "let's say someone asked you to breathe heavily. Could that be the beginning of hypnotizing you into an illusion?"

And he would be remembering what had happened following the conversation on the red phone in the presidential bathroom. He was asked to breathe deeply because he was too nervous and his breathing, while it could not be controlled, could approach regularity. And the three of them walked out and he had felt two hands on his waist and even the frail Oriental was lifting him with no effort. He smelled a faint perfume wafting up from the kimono and then it was like no smell at all, so subtle that it was free of scent.

They moved with a silence greater than quiet. There was water and heavy water and this silence that they all moved in was a greater silence than the stillness of a leaf. It was the silence of not existing so that when they came upon one of the Secret Service men from behind, they drew no more attention than a table. It was a strange feeling to be standing behind a man who did not know you were there.

The President did not see the hand move. But he did see the rustle of the kimono settling where the hand must have come from. The security man's head popped forward as though punished by a rolled-up magazine. The white man, called Remo, steadied the security man back into his chair.

"You didn't kill him, did you?" the President asked.

"Naah," said Remo. "He'll wake up in a few minutes and think he dozed off. Shhh. You gotta keep quiet. This hallway is loaded with eyes and ears. Your electronic stuff."

It was a dream moving, held by the two men in this world of silence, and in this world of silence, other sounds became more noticeable, sounds he would never again hear in these halls, like the whirring of machines. Later he would ask what machines they had in this hall and he would be told there were hidden cameras on motor mounts but that he couldn't possibly hear the motor working because it was like a mosquito at twenty yards.

"Does it go 'whir-a-boop, whir-a-boop'?" the President asked.

"Yes, but you've got to have your ear right next to it. And you'd have to get through a wall to get next to it."

So they moved in this silence, stopping every now and then, as if they were viewers to a performance on a stage where the actors could not see them. At a corner with a white painted arch and a gold eagle that would have been in poor taste anywhere but the White House, they paused. A printed wallpaper behind a large portrait of an American general from the Mexican-American war opened easily, like a wooden wound. Behind it was musty brown wood, with peeling old shellac like those old mansions back home in Georgia before they reconstructed them.

This was old American craftsman's shellac.

And the President moved into the long wood crack in the wall and he felt plaster rub against his back. And the crack closed off behind him and he was in darkness and then he felt himself being pressed, made into a thinner person. The walls came in on him so that his chest could not move out to breathe. He was being squeezed into a narrower and narrower crevice and he could not expand his chest. And being unable to expand his chest, he could not breathe. Nor did he scream and he did not know if the darkness that was around him now was his leaving of consciousness or the wall he was in.

His feet could not move, his hands could not move, even his airless mouth was forced open by plaster and dry wood strips pushing the jaw back.

He was going to die. He had trusted these two men and he was going to die for it, wedged motionless, suffocating, inside the walls of the house from which he was supposed to govern the country.

The red telephone had done it. It stood for everything he was against: illegality, surreptitiousness, the playing on the weaknesses and fears of men. That whole organization CURE was an ad-

47

mission that democracy did not work. He was being punished by the Almighty for doing what his better instincts told him was wrong.

And the President wondered if submariners felt this way, dying without air when the hulls caved at too great a depth. No, he had no regrets, and somehow even as his body retched, pinned inside this wall, he knew it was not the end. There was too much pain for the end.

And suddenly he was breathing again, big free gulps of air in a lighted office. It was the Oval Office and there was a click behind him and he did not see where the wall had opened to let them all inside.

"My lord," said the President in a hoarse gasp.

"Yes," said Chiun.

"The White House is a network of secret tunnels," the President said.

"No," said Chiun. "It has fewer than most palaces. There is not one that does not have these entrances. The pharaohs understood this."

And it was then that the President began to understand what world leaders had known before him. They were exceptional targets and the more important they were, the greater the attempts made upon their lives. The pharaohs had understood that great amounts of money could corrupt and the greatest sums were offered for their heads. They responded by removing the heads of their own chief architects whenever a palace was done to keep the palace secrets secret.

The castles of Europe were a joke. They had more secret entrances and exits than a modern football stadium. The President wondered whether Chiun would share this information with America's CIA.

The Master of Sinanju refused.

"Sinanju has been here for centuries. We will be here for centuries more. Before you were a country, we were. When you are gone, like the Roman Empire and the Ming Dynasty, we shall still be here. And we will still keep our secrets. Because a weakness kept secret remains a weakness. Once shared with someone else, it is usually corrected."

"I see where I have a lot to learn. It is not to my taste to use people like you, but I see where it is either you or death."

"What a misfortune," said Chiun, bowing his aged head. There were problems, he said. Great problems. There was an agreement he had with Emperor Smith and now he could not overturn that agreement lest the poor babies starve in Sinanju. However, if the President who was a far greater personage than Emperor Smith, should offer more money as tribute, then Chiun could not possibly refuse. His village would demand it. Besides, said the Master of Sinanju, he was tired of working for ugly men and wanted to work for a handsome emperor whose wisdom was appreciated throughout the world.

"Thank you," said the President. "But by working for Smith, you are working for me and all the American people."

Did the President trust Smith? Did the President know of Smith's ambitions late at night when each man imagines himself to be ruler of the country? If Smith had to die, were to die, then Chiun would be free to sign a new contract with the President. How much did the President really trust Smith? Already it was rumored,

Chiun said, that Smith was planning a drive to seize power. Did the President really trust Smith?

"Implicitly," said the President.

Well, allowed the Master of Sinanju, if the President wanted to entrust his life to any willy-nilly ambitious man from the North, who hated people from the South, who looked down on people from the South as inferior, who lusted after the President's wife, then the Master of Sinanju would do what he could do against such formidable odds.

"I never knew Smith looked down on anyone because of regionalism."

"He doesn't, Mr. President," said Remo.

"I must know what you're going to do. How do you propose to effect saving my life which many people now tell me is in some special danger for some reasons I don't understand. What and how are your methods?"

"Sorry, sir, but the House of Sinanju does not propose saving lives. It saves them. It does not share its methods with every two-hundred-year-old country. It is Sinanju. Everything else is less," Remo said.

"He does not mean that, oh, gracious American emperor," said Chiun. "We can help you better by easing the strain of knowledge upon you. Did you understand movement? No. Neither would you understand this. Just allow us to guarantee your life unconditionally."

And it was agreed. But the President looked older that evening because he had just accepted a hard reality—that there would have to be people in this world doing things in his name that he did not approve of.

Outside, Chiun allowed as how Remo was beginning to learn. He especially liked Remo's attitude toward new countries. But most of all was Remo's new ability to understand things without being told.

"Like what?" asked Remo.

"Like promising to save his life. We cannot do it, of course. Nobody can guarantee saving a life anymore than one can guarantee to make life. One can only guarantee a death."

"I intend to save his life."

"That makes me most sad," said Chiun. "I had thought you were becoming wise."

For, he explained, it was an old guarantee that one could give an emperor that his life would, without question, be saved. For if one failed, the only person who had heard the promise made—besides yourself—would no longer complain.

It was of little matter. And this Chiun tried to use to reassure Remo.

"The least endangered position in the entire world is that of your emperor or king."

"I thought everyone tried to kill them."

"That is true," Chiun said. "But has the death of one emperor ever meant that there would be no more? There is always someone willing to take that position in the world. And it is the least of all positions. Most attain it by entering the world from the correct womb. And what baby ever chose his womb or made an effort to be born? Yet that is how most emperors are made. It is the least position, while appearing to be the most."

Thus spoke Chiun on that spring night in Washington, D.C. Thus spoke the Master of Sinanju.

But his pupil was not quite as philosophical about the comings and goings of world rulers.

"I like this President, Chiun. I'm going to save him. Besides, I've seen the Vice President."

CHAPTER FOUR

The knife came very slowly. So did the man behind it. He jumped from a shiny black Buick LeSabre, his black shiny paratrooper boots clomping on the sidewalk.

"Whitey, you dies," he bellowed. He wore a towel around his head with a cheap orange glass jewel in the middle. "Die fo' Allah."

He was a big man, at least six feet four and 250 pounds, his face glowering with flaring nostrils.

"I'm busy," Remo said. And he was. They had left the White House through the front gate and been followed and Chiun was in the middle of explaining the politics of assassination, that there were many reasons for it, and only rarely did assassinations descend to the mindlessness of hate or revenge. Hate was to performance of a function as a boil on the heel was to the long jump. It was at best a distraction and, at worst, a crucial impediment.

And in the midst of this while Remo was trying to piece together the connection between an explosion in Sun Valley, Utah, and the presidential concern for assassination, some guy with a knife disturbed him by blocking the street in front of them.

"This ain' no niggah muggin'," snarled the man. "This a Muslim holy war o' righteousness."

"I'm very busy," said Remo.

"I Arab. I gots Arab name. Name Hamis Al Boreen. That mean savior of his people."

"That means nothing," said Chiun to Remo. Chiun knew Arabic and had once explained to Remo that the western word assassin came from Arabic, from the word hashish which assassins were supposed to use to give themselves courage. "Hashishan" had become "assassin." They were good, but not great, assassins. Often they did sloppy work. They killed unnecessarily and, what was anathema to Chiun, they had no qualms about killing children to obtain their ends. "That is not an Arab name," said Chiun.

"I Hamis Al Boreen," repeated the man. He raised his curved knife. He plunged his curved knife toward Remo's chest. Remo walked past the outside of the arm, so the lumbering oaf's thrust carried him by Remo and Chiun. An observer would think the man had merely stumbled through them, but no one could attack anything on the outside of his arm moving past him.

"There are two kinds of assassination. One is the vicious insane blood murder for revenge that is becoming increasingly common in your country. It is not even assassination. It is just killing. The other is the elegant, perfect function of a civilization at its peak, honoring its craftsmen. These are assassinations paid for in advance."

"Which one does the President have to fear?" Remo asked.

"All of them," said Chiun. "But there is a particular one coming to him and he does not see it."

The big man with the towel imitation of a turban and the imitation Arab name lifted his bulk back up to standing balance. Three others with towels also wrapped around the heads, one still carrying a Sears' white sale label, came to him from cars farther down the street. Obviously the first man was supposed to have stopped Remo and Chiun, diverting their attention, while the other three made the real attack. Now all four were running down the block after Remo and Chiun.

"Kill in de name of de all merciful and mighty," screamed the man as the four charged. They were in the worst positions to attack, Remo knew. The best stroke was a balanced stroke. It had more power. Running at something and swinging at it simultaneously appeared to be more powerful, but it was only an illusion. Power was balance and all four were off balance and running. The three helpers had machetes.

"There has been an example set for this emperor of yours," Chiun said.

"How did you know that, Little Father?"

"If one uses one's head and sees and hears instead of talking back, one can easily deduce there was a threat that your President failed to take seriously. But Emperor Smith did take it seriously and wanted the President to take it seriously, so he sent us. And we convinced him."

"But how did you know it's one threat? One particular threat?"

"Not only is it just one threat but the example was in your Sun Valley of Utah," said Chiun with not a little pride.

"How do you get to that, Little Father?"

55

"And they put you in charge?" sighed Chiun.

The attack by the four men was met with short sidestepping and rolling by as though Remo and Chiun were letting a dark rushing subway crowd push by them. This glancing collision accompanied screams about the greatness of God by the four attackers and how they were going to wash the streets with the blood of the invader infidels.

One of the attackers lost his Sears' white sale towel.

"Dey has dishonored my turban. Dey has dishonored my turban."

Remo and Chiun stepped over the struggling bodies of the four men.

"I am in charge, Little Father," Remo said. "How did you know Sun Valley? I mean, why Sun Valley?"

"The only logical place," said Chiun.

"You never even heard of Sun Valley," said Remo.

"Smith told me."

"In the hotel in Los Angeles, right? What did he say?"

"He said he was worried about the death that was an example."

"And then what?"

"And then he betrayed me by putting you back in charge."

"Well, what makes you think that it's one person or one group that's the danger?"

"It is a danger. One danger. It is the one we know about. There may be others. The important thing is that the name of the House of Sinanju does not become associated with your emperor because if another one of your emperors goes, it could shame the name of the House of Sinanju.

And it would not be our fault because your land is filled with insane bloody lunatics who do not get paid for this work."

Hamis Al Boreen and his crew regrouped for another charge.

"Stop or we cut," he threatened. "You ain' dealin' wif no ordinary niggers now. We all got Islamic names. Onliest people what can stop a Muslim is another Muslim, that who. It written in de holy whatchamacallit."

"I don't want this President to die, Little Father."

And Chiun smiled. "We all die, Remo. What you are saying is you do not wish his death to come too soon or too violently."

"Yeah. You've never listened to our Vice President."

"You mean if your President dies, his wife does not assume the throne?"

"No."

"Nor his children?"

"No."

"This Vice President, how is he related to the President?"

"He's not."

"He is not his son, this Vice President?"

"No," said Remo.

"Then we know who is behind this plot to assassinate, probably getting the work done for free too, so dishonorable is this person. He is the one who wishes your President dead. We will offer your President his head on a pole and be done with this dirty business where people kill others for free."

The four charged again, this time two coming in from each side. Since it appeared they were just going to keep it up and keep it up, Remo put one away with an elbow into the lower rib and another with a kick to the sternum and was about to finish the other two when Chiun said:

"Don't kill across me, please. It's very rude."

And with that the long-nailed fingers flicked out like a lizard's tongue and a small red spot appeared where an eye had been, the brain behind it jellied through the frontal lobe, and another hand caressed a wildly swinging blade so that its circular motion increased and with a thwuck stopped its motion in the man's own belly. The towel with the orange glass in the middle of it popped off the head. The eyes widened.

"Jesus Mercy," said Hamis Al Boreen who had discovered his new name while buying a Twenty Mule Team product by mistake when he had wanted cornstarch. After all, who ever heard of eating borax?

And then there was blood in his mouth and on his face and he could not stand.

"Okay, Sun Valley," said Remo. "It's a resort, you know."

"Will I meet the stars?" asked Chiun who followed American entertainers on television during the day. He had not been watching regularly lately, however, since these programs had, as he said, "abandoned decency." There was too much violence.

He bent down to pick up the orange-colored glass. He held it up to a street light.

"Glass," he said disdainfully. "Is nothing real? Why, it is a bad imitation. There is no orange jewelry in the entire world. This fraud is not even an imitation anything." Chiun kicked the corpse. "Violence. Violence in my daytime dramas

58

even. This is not a country worth saving. Your worst elements like human waste in one of your cesspools float to the top."

"You can watch the old shows, Little Father," said Remo, walking back in the night to the White House where they could get a cab to the airport.

"It's not the same. I know them all. I know the troubles of all the stars. The stars are not the same today. They have sex today. They punch people today. They talk obscenely today. Where are the good and innocent and pure?" asked Chiun, Master of Sinanju and lover of "As the Planet Revolves" which had gone off the air recently after twenty-five years. "Where is pure innocence and decency?"

"Where is it in life, Little Father?" asked Remo, not without a bit of wisdom.

"You are standing next to it," said Chiun.

There was no flight to Sun Valley until the morning, and while waiting at Dulles Airport Remo reflected on how many airports he had waited at for how many nights and how early he had given up the hope of ever having a home where he could rest his head and see the same people in the morning as he had seen the night before.

Instead he had something else, a oneness with the fullness of the use of his body that only a handful of people had ever had.

Because Remo was Sinanju, sharer of the sun source of all the martial arts, each like a ray from the original and the most powerful. And yet, there were too many nights in too many airports and he did not even have a home village to send money to. Chiun told him that Sinanju was his home, but that was a spiritual home if anything. Remo could not regard himself as an Oriental, as a Korean. He was an orphan, which was why Smith had chosen him as CURE's enforcement arm, and a long time ago made him disappear to become a man who didn't exist, working for an organization that didn't exist.

Airports were a place where people ate candy bars and drank coffee until morning. Or got drunk until the bars closed. Or read magazines.

He had an urge to scream in this swept and clean expanse of modern construction, waiting to let out its people to the drone airplanes that came up alongside to swallow them. It was a place for people passing through and it was his home. He was passing through life and was as secure as a man hurling himself off a four-story building. He remembered the morning before and the exercise and how his home was that time and space between birth of the leap and the perfect landing.

So be it, thought Remo.

He did not yell out.

The next day, a local policeman dozed in the heat as he sat on the corner foundation of what had once been a house. There was a hole in the ground where Ernest Walgreen had spent his last days trying to survive an assassination attempt.

Chiun looked down into the hole and smiled. He beckoned Remo. Remo looked down into the hole. He saw what was left of the foundation in pieces, the shattering that could come only from explosives implanted in the foundation itself.

"Well?" asked Chiun.

The guard blinked himself awake. He told the Oriental and the white man they weren't supposed to be there. They told him they would implant that shotgun on his lap into his chest cavity

60

if he continued to bother them. He saw the easy way the two moved, assumed they could do him harm, and went back to sleep. He had fifteen years to go before retirement, and he wasn't going to get there any faster by hassling troublemakers.

"Well?" Chiun said.

"Case closed," said Remo.

"Is there nothing new except deterioration?" bemoaned Chiun. "Such an old thing."

"My first lesson. One of them," said Remo. "The Hole. And there is even a hole here which is funny because at the end of 'The Hole,' if it's properly done, the hole disappears."

Remo remembered well. It was a story each Master passed to his successor. It was a technique to do work that had at one time seemed impossible. And it went like this:

Once, before Sinanju achieved its full power and when Masters often got killed in vain attempts to achieve their ends, there lived a shogun of Japan in a great castle. And one of his lords wished that he be removed so that the lord could become shogun and rule the land of Japan. It was a time even before the Samurai or the code of Bushido. For the Japanese, it was a very long time ago. For Sinanju, some time.

This shogun had brave followers. They always were by him, in rows of three. Three guarded three guarded three.

It was like a beehive and the shogun was the queen bee. He was most powerful. He lived in a great castle. Now the Master of Sinanju was not the strongest and it was before the full and total use of the breath was known. He was called The

Fly, because he would move quickly, then stop, quickly, then stop.

The Fly knew he could not kill the shogun in his castle. He was, being Sinanju, better than any Japanese fighter at that time. But he was not better than all of them added up. This was many many centuries before Ninji, the Japanese night-fighters who had learned by watching Sinanju and, of course, watching could only reproduce an imitation.

Now these were especially hard times for Sinanju and there was much hunger in the vil-lage. And the people looked to the Master and he could not tell them. "The shogun is too strong and I am too weak." You do not tell these things to babies. You tell starving babies: "Here is your food, loved one."

So that was what The Fly told them. He took part of the money payment from the lord who wanted the shogun dead and with it he bought food. The rest was to be delivered to the village when he succeeded.

The Master came to Japan by the sea. And such was the strength of this shogun that it was known right away that an assassin had come to kill him.

But even if there was not the full power in Sinanju at that early time, there was already the wisdom. And from the beginning, it had been known that for every strength there is a weakness and from every weakness a strength. Iron that will deflect an arrow will drown its wearer by pulling him under the water. Wood that floats crumbles in the hand. The thrown knife leaves its thrower without a weapon.

At the other end of life is death. And at the end of death, there must be life.

These things did The Fly know. And he knew he was being watched for the shogun had eyes in the very soil of Japan. In the sacred cities and the villages. Everywhere.

So The Fly pretended to drink too much wine. And when drinking, he knew one of the eyes of the shogun approached and he told him the secrets of strength, that for every strength there is a weakness. And he gave him the examples.

Right away this information reached the shogun. And the shogun right away demanded of the spy that he find out from The Fly what the weaknesses were in the shogun's strength.

And The Fly said that the walls were so thick commands could not be given through them and the men around the emperor were packed so tightly that a disloyal one must be among them. For among many is a better chance to have an evil one.

Now this shogun was known to buy whatever was the sharpest blade or strongest warrior. And he sent the spy back to ask The Fly what would be better than his castle or his many men. This, before he would kill The Fly.

And The Fly said there was a hole in which the greatest robber of all Japan hid and could not be caught.

Now there were always robbers in every land. Some lands had fewer. Lands that suffered had more. Being free of this criminal type meant only having fewer of them than others. There was never such a thing as no crime anywhere. So The Fly knew there had to be a robber somewhere, even in the orderly land of Japan. And there was.

And the spy asked, which robber do you mean? And The Fly answered:

"The great one so great the shogun does not even know his name. Nor can he ever find him. That is the safest man in all Japan. In the safest place because he cannot be betrayed there."

And when asked where that was, The Fly told the spy that only he and the great robber knew and he would not tell anyone because it was a promise to a dying man. The robber had lived and died peacefully and only the Master of Sinanju knew where this safest place was and he would carry that secret to his grave. He would never give away such a treasure.

And the spy the next day brought back jewels and asked to trade the jewels for the knowledge of the safe place. But the Master refused for he said the safety of the place would be lost if he told it to anyone who merely had money. For the safety was in its secrecy and only the user and the Master of Sinanju could know the place, for common knowledge of it would be like fire through a wood and paper palace.

He would only tell the man who was going to use it.

Now the shogun, being most Japanese, set his mind with discipline and fervor to unlock the mystery of the safest place in his kingdom. And the Master of Sinanju was taken to a place where torture was done to him and still he did not disclose the place, and finally to the shogun was he taken and there he did what no Japanese dared. He called the shogun a fool.

"You who are the power behind the emperor, you who have taken heads by the thousands, are the biggest fool in the land. You might as well set

64

yourself aflame as to continue on your foolish course. For if I told you the location of this safest place, you would not have a safe place but a place at the mercy of my torturers. Do you trust them with your life? After you have trusted my life to them?

"Lo, even now I cannot tell you because you are not alone. Guards upon guards are around you. You are not worthy of this safe place. I will take it to my grave with me."

And the Master of Sinanju was ordered taken from the great palace of the shogun to a small house by the sea where he was given nourishment and his wounds nursed. When he was well, he received a visitor alone just before sunrise. It was the shogun.

"Now, Master, you may tell me. I am worthy of it."

And The Fly demanded a great price for the location of this safest place for if he gave it away it would not be valued. For when man sets a price on something, he really sets his own value of it.

And the price was paid although the Master of Sinanju knew he could never claim it for the price was in land which led the shogun to believe The Fly intended to stay and live. But The Fly knew that once the shogun thought he had found the safest place, the Master would be killed so the shogun need fear no one's betrayal.

So the Master told the shogun to come to the outskirts of the sacred city of Osaka, three days hence, and from there they could walk in one night. The master named a spot for the meeting and said the shogun must come alone.

But of course the shogun did not. At a short distance were three faithful lords all with weapons. But none who would succeed the shogun if he died. Thus he could trust them more.

It was enough that the shogun was within arm's length. And the Master brought him to a little hill, and he said:

"Here it is. The place I spoke of."

And the shogun replied: "I see nothing."

"You are not supposed to," said the Master of Sinanju. "For if you saw something, so would others. That is why this is so safe. Take my sword. Dig."

"I am shogun. I do not dig."

"You cannot find it without digging. It is most spacious. But the entrance is sealed, can't you see. And I am still too weak from the cuts and burns of your torturers."

So the shogun dug with the Master's sword and he dug most of the night until there was a hole as high as his head. And when it was this high, the Master, who was not all that injured because there is a way to allow your body to be tortured so that things appear more painful and more harmful than they really are, lifted a great rock above his head. And he whispered:

"Shogun, you are now in the only safe place that has ever been in the world. The grave." And with that, the Master brought the rock crushing down on the shogun's head.

And he called to the three following lords who were now matched out in the open against a Master of Sinanju and he slew them, all did The Fly slay, one, two and three. And he took their heads and put them on poles and fled the land.

And when the lord who had bought the death of the shogun became himself shogun, he sent much tribute to Sinanju. Rice did he send and fish in great plentitude, and jewels and gold and swords. For during his reign, he used The Fly much and was considered the finest ruler Japan ever had.

This was how Remo had heard the story, and when he had looked up the new shogun's name, he had seen that the man had been one of Japan's bloodiest leaders, which made sense for anyone employing Sinanju so regularly.

The moral of the story was that if you can't get to someone where he's at, get him to where you can get at him.

Remo looked down into the shattered remains of the foundation.

"Explosives in the foundation itself, Chiun," he said. He jumped into the hole. He crumbled pieces of foundation in his hand.

"So whoever got this guy out here into this place probably acted like The Fly way back when. But why bother to get that guy here at all?"

"Who knows how whites think?" asked Chiun.

"I don't know, Little Father," Remo said. He was worried. And he became more worried when he found out, by checking back in Minneapolis, who had put Ernest Walgreen, businessman, into that Sun Valley house. It was a security agency.

"It doesn't make sense, Chiun. Now we know whoever put Walgreen here killed him. But why a security agency he hired to protect him?"

"You are jumping to conclusions," Chiun said. "Perhaps the security agency was tricked into bringing this Walgreen to Sun Valley. Would the story of The Fly have been any different if he did not go with the shogun himself to have him dig the hole, but had tricked someone else into doing

67

it? The lesson would be the same, the result the same. The shogun dead."

"I guess you're right," Remo said, strolling the neat lawns of the Minneapolis suburb where Walgreen had lived. "But I'm scared for the President. How are they going to get him into a hole? And who are they? Was there anything else Smitty told you?"

"Who remembers what liars say?" Chiun asked.

"Smitty isn't a liar. That's the one thing he's not."

"Not only is he a liar but a foolish one. He promised that I was in charge and before the emperor, your President, he withdrew that promise and shamed me."

"What did he say? Come on. What's the connection? What's the connection between the death of this Walgreen here and an attempt on the President's life?"

"It is quite obvious," said Chiun with a lofty smile. "What they both have in common is simple."

"What's that?"

"They are both white."

"Thanks for the big help, Chiun."

Remo tried to think as he gazed along the driveway that curled behind Walgreen's house, effectively opening it up to an attack from any side. The furniture inside the house was covered. There was a for-sale sign on the lawn, which was four days past being neatly cut. It was a home where Walgreen had lived the kind of life Remo could never live.

Remo could touch this house with his hands and yet he could never have it. He envied Walgreen what Walgreen had had when he was alive. Killers could never get Remo that way but Remo could never have this house, the family that had lived here, the life they had shared.

Across the street, a woman with very yellow hair looked at Remo and Chiun too often to be disinterested. Remo watched her leave her car.

She walked with a smooth voluptuous grace, accustomed to assaulting male eyes with her very appeal. A light blue silk dress clung over full breasts. Her lips were pulpy and glistened. She smiled as if she could stampede a football team with a wave of her hand.

"That's the Walgreen house," she said. "I couldn't help noticing you examining it rather closely. I am an investigator for the House Committee on Assassination Conspiracies and Attempts. Here's my identification. Would you mind telling me what you're doing here?"

Her hand produced a small leather foldover wallet. Inside the wallet was her photograph, looking quite somber and hardly sexy at all, and the Congressional seal on the identification. Pressed underneath the identification was a folded piece of paper which Remo removed.

"You're not supposed to see that," she snapped. "That's important Congressional correspondence. It's a privileged communication. It's a Congressional communication."

Remo unfolded the paper that had been wedged underneath the identification. It was on the stationery of Rep. Orval Creel, chairman of the House Committee on Assassination Conspiracies and Attempts, in parentheses (CACA). The note read:

My place or yours?

69

It was signed: *Poopsie.*

"What are you investigating?" asked Remo.

"I'll ask the questions," she said, snatching back the folded piece of paper. Her name, according to her identification was Viola Poombs. "Now what are you doing here?" she asked, reading from a card that told her to ask that.

"Planning to murder the Supreme Court, Congress, and all the members of the Executive Branch making more than $35,000 a year," Remo said.

"Do you have a pencil?" asked Miss Poombs.

"Why?" asked Remo.

"So I can write down your answers. How do you spell planning."

"What did you do before you became a Congressional investigator?" asked Remo.

"I was a model in a finger-painting parlor," said Miss Poombs. Her billowing pinkish cleavage rose proudly and smelled moist in the spring heat. "But then Representative Creel made me an investigator. The problem for me is I don't know the difference yet between a murder and an assassination."

"In this degenerate country, child, you wouldn't," Chiun said. "But you will know. I have decided to teach you. Of all your kind, you will understand the difference best of all. Your committee will have wisdom and you, among your kind, shall be venerated as wise."

"My kind? What kind is my kind?" asked Miss Poombs.

"The billowy breasted white person," said Chiun, as if he were describing a bird he had seen on a winter meadow walk.

"That's cute," said Viola.

"Come on, Chiun, I'm working," Remo said. "You're not going to teach anybody anything."

"You're not cute," said Viola. "You're nasty." She glared at Remo and added, "I always wanted to be loved for my mind."

Remo looked at her chest. "Both of them?"

CHAPTER FIVE

Viola Poombs was all excited. She was going to find out who killed everybody. And the nice little Oriental man, why he was telling her so many things, nobody ever knew so many things about assassination, why Poopsie and his committee would just love to know everything. Everything! He might even run for senator and governor and then there would be better jobs than just being an investigator, she might even get to be vice governor or whatever one gets to be when they are close to their governor.

But first she had to do some things.

"With your clothes on?" asked the nasty white man called Remo.

"I wasn't going to take them off. I never take off my clothes in public. I'm not an exhibitionist. I am an employee of the federal government of the United States of America and I would take off my clothes only upon a direct order from a duly elected representative of the American people."

And that showed him. All right, maybe he knew more about killings and things but she had her rights too. And she was cooperating enough.

She had called the Secret Service and made an appointment with the assistant director, and he said he would see her. And they all went to Washington, and they were all going to see this man and they would ask questions. Important questions. Viola Poombs knew they were important because she was told she wouldn't understand them. That could mean only one of two things: either they didn't want to tell her or she really wouldn't understand them. Most things she didn't understand. What she did know was that you asked for things when men were all excited and that was the best time. Afterwards, when they were comfortable and released, that was the worst time.

It was not much that Viola understood but that simplicity had earned her, at twenty-four, the beginning of a $78,000 pension fund, 3,000 shares of Dodge-Phillips, $8,325.42 in a passbook account, and at least two years at $28,300 a year from the American taxpayers. She rightly understood that her good years were between now and thirty. Between now and then she would have to learn to do something with her mind. Unless she got married. But marriage was not that easy nowadays, especially considering that she looked for someone with more financial solvency than she had.

The thing she had to do before any of them stepped into the office of the assistant director of the Secret Service was to call the chairman of the committee she worked for.

"Hello, Poopsie," she said when Congressman Creel's secretary finally got her through. The secretary had been trying to learn to work the phone buttons for months now, but every time she had it almost down pat, she would have to take time off to prepare for another contest. Next year, she hoped to be Miss Walpole, Indiana.

"I'm in Washington," said Viola.

"You're not supposed to be in Washington. We're supposed to meet this weekend in Minneapolis. Remember the tip? That the killing of that Walgreen is somehow connected with presidential assassinations? That's why I sent you out there."

"I'm investigating. And I'm going to make you famous. You're going to know everything there is about assassinations."

"The only thing I have to know is how to get more money for my committee."

"There's money in assassinations?" asked Viola.

"Fortunes. Don't you look at the bookstands and the movies and the TV shows?"

"How much money?" asked Viola Poombs.

"Never mind," snapped Congressman Creel. "Get back to Minneapolis and watch that house. Or don't watch it. But get back there for when we arrive."

"How much money?" asked Viola, who in subjects like these refused to be intimidated.

"I don't know. Some guy just got $300,000 from a publisher for *Cry Mercy*. It's about how America's rotten greed caused all these assassinations, dear."

"You said three hundred thousand dollars?" repeated Viola slowly.

"Yeah. Now get back to Minneapolis, dear."

"Paperback or hardcover?" asked Viola. "Who kept the foreign rights? What about the movie share? Did anyone mention television spinoffs? Book clubs? Was there book club money?"

"I don't know. Why is it you become so damned technical when it comes to the almighty dollar? You're a greedy person, Viola. Viola? Viola? Are you there?"

Viola Poombs heard her name coming from the telephone earpiece as she hung up.

She left the booth in the Treasury building and went right up to the cute little old Oriental and gave him a big kiss on his adorable cheeks.

"Do not touch," said Chiun. "If you want to touch, touch him." He pointed to Remo. "He likes it."

"Are you ready, Miss Poombs?" asked Remo with a bored sigh.

"Ready," said Viola.

"The first thing you must remember," said Chiun as they all walked to the elevator, "is that assassinations have gotten a bad name in this country because of amateurism. Amateurism, free wanton murder without payment, is a curse to any land. I am telling you this so you will get it all right for your committee and everyone will know the truth, because I think I am going to be blamed if something goes wrong. And it will, because I am not in charge."

"Chiun," said Remo, "knock it off."

The assistant director of the Secret Service directed the President's safety. He never met anyone in his office because his office had charts of men in charge of assignments, White House protection, traveling protection and, worst of all, crowd control and protection.

The assistant director was forty-two years old and looked sixty. He had white hair, deep lines around his mouth and eyes, and deep dark water-melon wedges under his eyes, that always seemed to be staring out at some horror.

He sipped Alka Seltzer as he talked, washing down specially pressed bars of Maalox. The Maalox soothed his stomach. It took the great amount of acid his body poured into his intestines and neutralized it. His entire oral function was to combat these massive amounts of stomach acid his body produced during tension. While others sometimes got up in the middle of the night to urinate, he would wake up reaching for his Maalox. He dreamed in code.

When he first took over the job of protecting the President of the United States, he reported to the doctor that he was having a nervous break-down. The doctor told him he was doing better emotionally and physically than his predecessors had. For his job there were new standards for nervous breakdowns.

"New standards?" he asked. "What are they?"

"When you start peeling off pieces of your cheeks with a letter opener, then we begin to consider nervous breakdown. And we're not talking just outer layer either. A good gash, right down to bone. Last fellow ground down his teeth till they hit stubs."

So when the luscious blonde and the Oriental and the incredibly-relaxed American in black tee shirt and gray pants and a loose manner of lounging in a chair asked the key question, the morning's Maalox came up all over the confer-ence table.

"I take it," said Remo, "that there is a con-nection between the death of the Minneapolis businessman by explosion in Sun Valley and the safety of the President of the United States."

The Secret Service man nodded, wiping his lips with a handkerchief before the stomach bile ate through them to his gums. He quaffed a long gulp of Alka Seltzer and swallowed a Maalox bar whole. His lower intestines felt as if they were being crisp fried in Wesson oil. Much better, he thought.

"Direct connection. And we're worried. The way Walgreen was killed leads us to believe that we're facing a new level of assassin, probably the best there is."

"No. We are on *your* side," Chiun said.

"What?" asked the assistant director.

"Nothing," said Remo. "Ignore him."

"Are you sure you're from the House CACA committee?"

Viola Poombs showed her card again. The Secret Service man nodded in rhythm with his twitch.

"All right. Direct connection. Absolutely direct. If it weren't for the President of the United States, Ernest Walgreen and his wife would be alive today. How's that for direct?"

"Explain," said Remo.

"Explain," said Viola, because it sounded like the official thing to say.

"Don't bother," said Chiun. "It is obvious."

"How do you know?" demanded the Secret Service man.

"Because it is only done every other century," said Chiun disdainfully. And in Korean, he explained to Remo that it was a variation of The Hole. When one wanted tribute from an emperor not to kill him, one chose someone very well pro-

77

tected and killed him. This was not done by the House of Sinanju, because basically it involved collecting moneys for not doing work, and that cost the body its skills. To get paid to do nothing produced weakness and weakness produced death.

Remo nodded. He understood more and more Korean nowadays, but only the northern dialect of Sinanju.

"What did he say? What did he say?" asked the assistant director.

"He said there's somebody demanding tribute," Remo said.

"That's right. How did he know? How? How?"

"It's old stuff," said Remo. "Who gets the tribute and how much?"

"I can't say. The President has to authorize it and this new one, he didn't understand what it was and cancelled the payments. It's happened before, but before we could always get the President to listen. This guy won't even listen. He says he's got a country to worry about."

"You say it happened before. What before?" Remo asked.

"Well, before they threatened the President's life. The last President. They got hold of this loonie and gave her a .45 caliber gun and got her close, told her just how to get close, and then, if that wasn't enough, they got hold of a second loonie with a gun that went off and they said the next time, that would be it, so the White House paid off."

"How long has this been going on?"

"Since Kennedy's death. That was the end of the good old days." The assistant director's hands quivered and he got the glass up to his lips and most of the liquid in his mouth. He wore white

78

gray shirts with a crust design so the spilled Alka Seltzer and crushed Maalox would not show. "Being in charge of the President's safety is like using a bomb for a pillow. You can't sleep."

"All right," Remo said. "So the President has cancelled the payments. What happened since then?"

"We've gotten word that the President is going to be killed."

"Who sent you that word?"

"A phone call. Male. Late forties. Maybe Southern. Raspy voice. No trace of who he is."

"Start the payments up again. That should stop him," Remo said.

"We've thought of that. But we don't know how to reach the guy. Suppose he's just decided that it's time to kill a President? For whatever reason. Maybe he's tossed his cork. Who knows?"

"Any reason to think that?" asked Remo.

"Just one. He told us he was going to kill somebody as a lesson, before killing the President."

"And that was Walgreen," Remo said.

"Yeah." The assistant director nodded. "And you know who Walgreen was?"

"A businessman," said Remo.

"Right. And a former Secret Service man. And after he got out of the service, he was called back for a special occasional assignment."

"Which was?"

"Delivering the tribute money to prevent the presidential assassination," the assistant director said. "When he got killed, it was more than just an example to us that the assassin could kill. He killed the man who was directly responsible for getting the money to him. That's what scares me. It's like he's telling us I've got enough money

79

now, and this time I don't want money, I want the President's ass." The man grabbed again for the glass of Alka Seltzer.

Chiun flicked the glass from his quivering hand.

"Fool. Stop this. Stop this what you do to yourself."

"I'm not doing it. The job's doing it."

"You are doing it. And I will prove it," said Chiun. "When there is a death in the family, do you quiver like this?"

"I'm not responsible for keeping my family alive."

"You are, but you do not know it. You suffer from what you do know. You know your job is important and almost impossible. So you worry. *You.*"

"How the hell can I stop?"

"By accepting the simple fact that you cannot guarantee your success, and by thinking of your President as an egg. You will protect him just as well but you wouldn't worry about an egg, would you?"

The Secret Service man reflected for a moment, and then his body eased its chemical assault upon his stomach and a great relief came upon him. He thought of the President as an egg and suddenly felt an ease which no chemical had been able to bring to him. He felt exorbitantly good by, for the first time in months, not feeling extraordinarily bad.

Viola Poombs had gotten lost through the conversation between Remo and the assistant director and had stopped taking notes with a borrowed pencil on a borrowed pad. "The President is going to die?" she asked now. She wondered if she could get a book done, predicting it. Maybe something about exactly how it was going to be done. Perhaps some sex. She could pose nude in the centerfold. Perhaps a foldout centerfold of a book. She would need a connection between the nude picture and the very modest and religious President. Well, she would write the book herself. That was connection enough. Authors often had their pictures on book covers. Hers would be in the centerfold. Men didn't need too great an excuse to look at bareass pictures. And she had the ass to bare.

When Viola Poombs asked the question, the Secret Service man thought of his President being assassinated and he dove for the bottle. But a long delicate fingernail somehow miraculously stopped his progress.

"Think of egg. All your worry does not help. Only hurts. Think of egg," said Chiun.

The man did. He imagined an egg being broken by a sniper's bullet, cracked splat everywhere by a .45 caliber bullet. An exploding egg. A burning egg. A fried egg. An egg sandwich. Who cared about eggs? He felt better. He felt tremendous.

"Kind sir, how can I thank you?"

"Stop spreading lying slander about the House of Sinanju."

"House of Sinanju? Why I didn't say anything about that. And it's just a legend anyway."

"It is no legend. They are the wisest, kindest, most venerable assassins ever to grace this meager planet. Stop calling others 'possibly the best there is.' You insult the best when you call others the best. Know you this, trembling young man, the House of Sinanju can tame and humble these upstarts. Best? Hah, would you compare a sewer with all the oceans of the world? Then do not compare murderous knaves with the House of Sinanju."

"Who are you, sir?" asked the assistant director, tears of gratitude in his eyes.

"An unbiased observer," said Chiun. "One who has an interest in truth."

Outside the office, Chiun looked grave. A few paces from Viola Poombs, where she could not hear, he confided in Remo:

"We are in trouble. We must leave. Doom is near."

Remo hadn't noticed anyone making a move. He looked around.

"Remo, we cannot afford to allow the House of Sinanju to become associated with this pending disaster. What will the world think if your President is hacked to bits or exploded or shot in the head and the House of Sinanju was not only not the one which achieved it, but had instead been hired to protect him? It is bad, Remo. Countries come and go, but the reputation of Sinanju is important."

"Chiun, there are maybe fifty people in the entire world who have heard of Sinanju and forty-seven of them live there."

"Your President is going to die and embarrass us. That is what your President is going to do to us. If it were not against my ethics, I would kill him myself from the anger I feel. How dare he get himself carelessly killed to disgrace our name? It is true what they say about new countries being bad countries."

"What's this doom? What makes you so sure that he is going to die?"

"Did you not hear? Did you not listen? For years, your country was paying tribute for its fear. Tribute to others when the House of Sinanju was in their midst. Nevertheless, people do not pay tribute for nothing."

"They do it all the time," Remo said. "Ask a real estate broker. They sell one part house, three parts lying."

"But not governments with so many policemen and military men wishing to show their leaders how effective they are. This does not happen unless his protectors know in their hearts that they cannot save him. Every payment is a disgrace to them. This is so, Remo. Yet they have recommended paying off this murderer because they know he is capable of doing what he has threatened. For years they paid him. And then he killed the man who was the messenger of the money. This Walgroon."

"Walgreen," Remo said.

"Whatever. These killers killed him. They did not do that because they want more tribute. They did that because they are going to kill your President and they want his protectors to know that they cannot protect him."

Viola Poombs bounced over, her cleavage preceding her like ship's bells in fog.

"Everything all right?" she asked.

Remo did not answer. Chiun smiled.

"In your account of how this President died, you should note most of all he refused to avail himself of the House of Sinanju," Chiun said.

"Ignore him," Remo said. "This President *is* using the House of Sinanju. And the House of Sinanju will save him. I guarantee it. So get this down for the ages. The Master of Sinanju promises that no harm will befall the President. Be sure to write that down. It's important."

"Until this moment, Remo, I had not realized how cruel you were," Chiun said.

"I just want to give you some incentive, Little Father, for hanging around and protecting the Man."

"You are an evil person," Chiun said.

"Right," agreed Remo. "Did you get that, Viola?"

"Almost. How do you spell *guarantee?* And do you have a pencil I could borrow?"

CHAPTER SIX

Les Pruel of Paldor Security watched the blade
come down on the glistening sweaty neck of the
boy. The boy was about twelve and had a clubbed
foot, and two guards in resplendent uniforms had
pushed him down to his knees while the President
for Life of the Peoples' Democratic Republic of
Umbassa talked on about security and what sort
of guarantees could Mr. Pruel give that his excellency would not succumb to the fate of so many
African leaders.

"I can't, your highness. No one can. But I can
give you the best protection that technology and
our experience can offer. We at Paldor appreciate
your problems and we have never lost a client
yet."

"Never?" asked the President for Life.

The blade came down with a swish and then
the thunk of a cantaloupe being macheted in half.
The neck had gone first, then the throat, which
was why most executioners put the victim's head
facing down, so that the blade would hit bone
first at the strongest part of its stroke. The boy's
head rolled.

Well, thought Pruel, *his wretched life is over at least. To live in this kingdom is to live too long.*

Maybe he had lived too long. He had been mightily depressed since Paldor had lost Ernest Walgreen. Ernie had been with the Secret Service also. That house in Sun Valley had been safe. He was sure of it. And yet he could not stem the nagging torturous thought that he had led the former agent to his death. He had put him in that house as surely as if he had put him on top of a bomb.

It was a stupid move. You led people to safe exits and hideaways, not to bombs. He had brooded about this for weeks in the Paldor offices until the chairman of Paldor, the only member of the top-ranking staff who had never been with the Secret Service, called him in and said:

"Pruel. We got two kinds of people. Those who sell Paldor and those who don't work here anymore. Now I'm not having a mope around here anymore because no business needs a mope. We need sell. That's S-E-L-L, sell, and by toozit's dustwhumpher I mean sell."

Which was how Sylvester Montrofort talked. And when Mr. Montrofort talked, people listened. He had taken the dispirited band of Secret Service men after Kennedy's death and put them all on salary, which he paid himself, and talked to them and nursed them along until they all were wealthy businessmen. He had given them pride again. Motivation again. He had convinced them they had something worth selling and they should now get a good price for it. And they did. Les Pruel couldn't remember when he'd looked on the right side of a menu at the prices. Now he only looked at what might please him.

"Difference between rich and poor ain't in the

head, Pruel," Mr. Montrofort had once said. "It's in the hard honest dollars. That's the difference. Don't let anybody anytime tell you you're poor 'cause you think poor. You're poor 'cause you don't have two clinking nickels to rub together. That's poor. Rich is folding money, lots of it, and enough for whatever you want. Poor's not getting what you want. Rich is. That's the difference. All this stuff about what you think isn't worth the fuzz on a ten-year-old tennis ball. Shoot, if thinking was all that made you rich, damned hypnotists would be the richest ditwallers in the whole world. And they ain't. I ought to know. I know about that stuff."

Nobody ever really argued with Sylvester Montrofort. He had no legs and his back humped up in some spinal deformity, yet he could convey such enthusiasm that he could convince you that you and he could be a relay team in the Olympics.

So in the depression that set in after they lost Ernie Walgreen, Mr. Montrofort not only did not share the sadness but said it was time when good salesmen showed their stuff. Anyone could sell an oil well to a gas company, he said. But try selling a dry hole. Now, that's a salesman.

Les Pruel couldn't break the slump so Mr. Montrofort had shipped him off to Umbassa.

"Sell the gadgets. They love gadgets. Shiny gadgets," Mr. Montrofort had said.

"They can't use them."

"Shoot. If they want 'em, sell 'em. You can't sell training anymore. They know they got people who can't even use their thumbs. Sell gadgets. Radar."

"Radar is only good for airplanes."

"Tell him some other jungle bunny is going to

bomb him. I'll sell a couple of planes to his neighbor. Go ahead."

And he was in Umbassa. And the President for Life of The Peoples' Democratic Republic of Umbassa wanted radar. Lots of radar. The radar with the shiny buttons. So he could shoot down airplanes in the sky all over the world.

Les Pruel had to explain that radar didn't shoot down planes. It just showed you where they were so they could not sneak up on you and kill you while you slept in your palace, surrounded by your faithful field marshals and generals and supreme generals and commanders for eternity. That's what radar was for.

The President for Life wanted the kind of radar that shot down planes all over the world.

There was no such thing, said Pruel.

"The Russians will sell it to me," said the President for Life.

"Oh," said Pruel. "You mean the destabilizer. That's the one where you can never be killed by a bomb dropped from above. But it has its problems."

"What problems?" asked the President.

"It is used to save only one person. The entire network can save only one person in a country. Do you have such a person, who must be saved, even though the whole country should perish?" asked Pruel.

They did have such a person.

It was the President for Life, of course. And Pruel set up the phony system next to the planes that Umbassa pilots could not fly. It was $440 worth of old hifi and television equipment, polished to a glistening shine. There was an old Zenith radio grid. Paldor craftsmen cut out the form of a bomb from sheet metal. They put a tiny battery under it and a bulb in it. The bulb was red. It blinked.

The President for Life was supposed to keep the tiny protective device in his pocket all the time and he would never be hit by a bomb. It cost $2,300,000. Less than even one of the cheap Russian planes.

The President for Life promptly told an American reporter how he had, through technological ingenuity, purchased an air defense system cheaper than a single plane. But it was a military secret and he would not tell the reporter what it was, only that he could never be hit by a bomb. He kept his hand in his pocket all through the interview.

In gratitude, the President of Life gave Les Pruel a sword. But he would not think of giving it to him unblooded, for that was an insult. So he ordered the sword and someone brought the boy who dragged his foot and Les Pruel watched the head roll and he knew then that he was not going to work for Paldor anymore. He had become one of Sylvester Montrofort's salesmen and he didn't like it in himself. He didn't like the product, if and when a real product existed. He didn't like the customers. He didn't like himself.

"You look unhappy," said the President for Life. "You do not understand. It is a fine sword. We have many young boys and that one was useless. We are moving in giant steps to technology and therefore they become even more useless."

"They, who?" asked Pruel. He thought of Ernie Walgreen.

"The children who will grow up to join workers' brigades. We sell them if you want to buy them, although in your country, you cannot do that with your capitalist laws."

Les Pruel forced a smile and thanked the President for Life and declined an offer to try the sword himself. It was wrapped in velvet by facile black hands. Pruel didn't want to look at eyes anymore. He watched the hands.

"Paldor wishes his excellency, President for Life, a long and safe life."

"Better than Russian radar," said the President for Life, patting his pocket. "Now we do not have to shoot down planes because they can do us no harm. Let them drop atomic bombs. We are safe. Safe from the world. Safe from the crazed hateful Zionist hordes who wish to enslave the world."

"Yes. An honored client of Paldor," said Pruel.

"Do you have something that could make me safe from bullets?"

"No," said Pruel, for he knew the President for Life would try it out on another young boy.

"I would test this wonderful device but it might get lost in someone else's pocket. Two million dollars is too much to entrust to anyone but me, yes?"

By evening, Les Pruel was on an Air Umbassa jet. It was made by McDonnell Douglas, flown by French pilots, serviced by West German mechanics. Umbassa's three female college graduates were the stewardesses. Thy could read instructions with only a little help.

As part of Umbassa's drive for education, they were all pronounced doctors and, after they slept with the President for Life, given Ph.D. degrees. Two of them could count to ten with their fists closed, although one did confess that when she was going as high as ten, it helped to visualize her fingers.

Les Pruel did not want coffee, tea, or milk. He didn't want a drink.

"Is there anything you do want?" asked the stewardess.

"I want to like myself again." said Pruel.

And with wisdom that was almost shocking in its clarity, she said, "Then you must stop liking someone else better."

"You're pretty smart," said Les Pruel. "You're very smart."

"Only because you do not know what I know. You seem smart to me because you know things I do not know," said the stewardess.

Les Pruel closed his eyes but had a disturbing dream. He was watching a Punch and Judy puppet show. Punch grabbed a knife. Punch suddenly lunged out at Les Pruel but went right by him into a fire and was consumed. The horror was that Punch had Pruel's face. He was the puppet and he was going to try to kill but be killed in the process.

During a previous fit of depression, he had seen an analyst and learned to work out dreams, which meant finding out what you were trying to tell yourself. But what was he telling himself? Was he a puppet? He woke up screaming.

"Mr. Pruel. Mr. Pruel." It was the stewardess. She was calming him. He said he had had a bad dream. She warned him that when one was high above the earth and traveling, one should take one's dreams very seriously.

"You believe strange things about dreams but we know they tell the future," she said. "Especially when you dream on a high place. Beware."

"I'd beware, but there's nothing to beware about," he said, laughing. And then he had a drink and felt good.

He had enough to retire quite comfortably, not luxuriously perhaps, but enough to feed him and his family and any work was better than watching heads roll and selling useless items to illiterate murderers.

He didn't wait for the jet lag to clear. His mind was clear enough without recovering from that mental and physical malady that afflicts international travelers.

It was noon in Washington when the plane landed and it was one o'clock when he walked up the ramp to Sylvester Montrofort's office. The office had hydraulically controlled levels to make the visitor sit at any level Mr. Montrofort wanted. It was not that Mr. Montrofort wanted the visitor to sit beneath him to exert power; it was that Mr. Montrofort wanted the visitor to feel secure and superior when looking down at Montrofort, if the sale proved too easy. Made a tough sell, Mr. Montrofort would sometimes say. Sometimes selling was too easy for the seller, unless he gave the sellee the edge.

Unshaven, striding hard, jaw set, Les Pruel marched into Montrofort's office.

"Mr. Montrofort, I quit," he boomed.

The gnarled ratlike face and dark powerful eyes of Sylvester Montrofort were infused with a sudden joy. He smiled the best smile modern dentistry could sell. He pressed a button on his wheelchair.

Les Pruel watched the wheelchair and Mr.

Montrofort sink below him, as if the floor was built on quicksand. When Mr. Montrofort's hairless head was level with Pruel's knee, the floor stopped dropping.

"Go to it, boy. I haven't had a tough sell for a damned pine picket's week."

"I don't want to work here anymore, Mr. Montrofort."

"I got a ten-year contract out there with my secretary and it's going to have your name on it by the time you leave this office, Pruel. I like the cut of your timbers, boy. Dammit, you think I'm going to give up on someone who can sell four hundred dollars' worth of old television and victrola parts for more than two million dollars? Boy, you're not getting away from me. I love you. That's L-O-V-E. Love."

"I can spell, Mr. Montrofort. Q-U-I-T. That's quit."

"Well, something is bothering you and it shouldn't. You've got the greatest job and the greatest company and the greatest future in the world. You'll never be happy anywhere else so let's you and me work this out together. You're more than an employee-stockholder with option benefits. You're the life of this company and when you stop breathing with us, we all die a little bit. So what's the problem?"

"Ernie Walgreen. We lost him and we shouldn't have. I'm so damned busy selling that I've forgotten I was trained to protect people. I used to be proud of that. I was proud of what I did. I'm not proud anymore, Mr. Montrofort." Les Pruel felt good saying that. He looked at his hands. He felt the relief of tears come upon him. "When I earned what I would hardly even count now, when I worked to protect the President, when I couldn't afford to take my family to a restaurant, I was still proud. I was proud of my job. Even when we lost Kennedy, I felt bad, but I was proud because we had done the best we could. Mr. Montrofort, I'm not proud anymore."

The bald head came up above the floor level, the dark fiery eyes next, the nose that looked as if it had been put on in pale cracked pieces, and the mouth with the perfect set of teeth, like a mouth transplanted from a twenty-year-old toothpaste model. The tortured humped shoulders rose above Pruel's kneeline. The wheels of Mr. Montrofort's chair appeared. Then his face was level with Pruel's and Montrofort was not smiling.

It was then that Les Pruel realized he had never before dealt with Sylvester Montrofort when the man wasn't smiling or harrumphing or old-boying himself into a sale.

"I've never been proud, Pruel," said Montrofort. A large drop of sweat quivered over his earlobe and then descended like a viscosity convention all voting simultaneously that it was too hard to stay on the side of this man's face anymore. Pruel watched it go.

This was the first time Sylvester Montrofort wasn't selling him something. With great effort, Montrofort lifted a quart bottle of dark liquor out of his lower desk drawer. He lifted out two glasses in one hand and poured two big drinks.

It was not an offered drink, it was an ordered drink.

"Okay, you're through. Drink that. You got some listening to do."

"I know you've had problems, Mr. Montrofort."

"Problems, Pruel? No. More like crucifixions.

You ever see that extra big smile when someone meets you for the first time and you know it's a be-nice-to-the-gnome kind of grin. He's smiling because he's really repulsed by you. And women? What do you think I have to do to have normal relations with a woman? I am not just your average person like anyone else who happens to have a handicap. That I am gnarled and cannot walk is the most important thing about me. Crippled dwarf. That's what I am. Don't tell me I'm a handicapped person. I am not a person. I am a crippled dwarf and a horror to you people. You're a person. I'm a mutant. If the proper selection process had worked, I would not have been able to reproduce. You see, that's how species survive. Mutants, inferior weaklings like me, do not reproduce."

"But you're not inferior. Not in your mind or your will," said Pruel. Mr. Montrofort looked hunched over his frail body, as if sheltering a painful stomach. He nodded for Pruel to drink.

The liquor tasted very sweet, like syrup. Yet it had a sharpness to it, as if someone had infused a tangy citrus in it, an almost overhwelming grape-fruitiness. It overflowed him with good feeling. He wanted more. He finished his glass and then surprisingly he had Montrofort's glass in his hand and was sipping that.

"Pruel, I am a freak. I have a better mind than yours and a stronger will than yours but I am not you. I am better than you. I am worse than you. And most of all, I am other than you. You've lived a little too well for an ex-cop. That's all you Secret Service men are. Ex-cops."

"Yes. Ex-cop," said Pruel.

"I never told you what it was like, Pruel, to be a

95

crippled dwarf and watch all the bosomy ladies go by. I didn't have even one leg, but I had a double dose of lust. And so what does a man do when he is repulsive to women? How does he slake that great thirst? He becomes the best salesman you've ever seen."

"Yes, the best," said Pruel. He finished the wonderful glass of liquid and got up and snatched the bottle from Montrofort. It was his bottle. It was good. The world was good.

"You loved Ernest Walgreen," said Montrofort.

"Loved," said Pruel. He drank from the bottle. The bottle was good. Good was the bottle.

"You will kill his killers."

"Kill his killers," said Pruel. He was going to do that.

"You are an avenging angel."

"Angel. Avenging."

"You will put bullets into two men. One is white and one is Korean. You will be shown where they are. Here are pictures. They are with a blond woman with excruciatingly lovable breasts, with mounds of luscious glory preceding her like trumpets before the Lord."

"Kill," said Pruel, and the grapefruity taste filled his body. He had just gone through the very good feelings of nice boozy comfort and now he was clear about things. He knew who had killed Ernest Walgreen. Good old Ernie whom he loved. The two guys in the picture Mr. Montrofort had just shown him.

He had felt bad because he had not killed the two in revenge. If he were to kill them, all would be right again. He was above feeling good. Feeling good was for people who did not know the one good and great thing that would set everything right. The thing that had to be done. The one purpose for which a man lived. He knew what it was. His purpose was to kill. Those two men. Who were with a woman with big boobs.

Les Pruel hadn't felt right since Walgreen's death. The sticky itch of Umbassa was still with him, the feel of clothes left on your body too many days without air cleansing the pores.

It didn't matter. When he first tasted the drink, there was the warm goodness of a nice boozy mellow glow that filled him. But as he progressed, he rose above the need for feeling good. Feeling good was a crutch. Not to have to feel good was even better.

Was that Mr. Montrofort saying goodbye? It had to be. He was outside now and the sun was hot and the streets of Washington were hot and he felt he was going to vomit up all the grapefruit that had ever been grown. He felt lumps grow in his body. He saw the sun. It buzzed around his head and he smelled grapefruit orchards all around and his head hit something very hard. Crack.

Hands, soft hands pressed soft things to his head and he felt tremendous pain. But the pain did not matter.

He wished he had felt that way back in training. The laps they had to run while training for the Secret Service. He hadn't thought he was going to make it.

A very loud shot rang out near his ear. The sun disappearing. Someone was rubbing cold things on his head. He was thirsty. They gave him water. He wanted grapefruit. They didn't have grapefruit, but after he righted the wrongs against Ernie Walgreen, there would be that grapefruit drink.

"Shoot the kid," said a voice.

"Right," said Pruel. Where was his gun, he asked. You couldn't shoot without a gun.

"We will give you a gun that never misses," said the voice.

A woman screamed. Why did she scream?

"That man killed a child. He shot a child."

She pointed at him.

"Kill the woman," came the voice.

There. Now she wasn't screaming anymore. And this was right because everyone was right in front of the new J. Edgar Hoover building and there were the two men who killed Ernie Walgreen. The American with the high cheekbones and the dark eyes and the Oriental in the kimono.

He heard the voice again and now he knew the voice was not outside his head, but inside. He would listen to the voice and he would do what it said and make everything right and have peace and wonder for all time.

"Kill the Korean," said the voice.

The Korean fell with a fluff of the kimono.

"Kill the white," came the voice.

And the white man fell, spinning helplessly in his black tee shirt.

"Good," said the voice. "Now kill yourself."

And then Les Pruel saw that indeed he had a gun. It was a rifle and had a barrel and way down the barrel was his hand squeezing the trigger.

But what about the grapefruit?

And what about the big-boobied blonde screaming her head off?

What about the nice crippled Mr. Montrofort and his sexual problems?

And Ernie Walgreen? Good old Ernie Walgreen? What about him?

"Pull the trigger," came the voice.

"Oh, yes. Sorry," said Les Pruel.

The .30 caliber slug came up into his cheekbone like a truck going through a watermelon. The bone splattered, the ethmoidal sinus ruptured into the olfactory bulb, which meant Les Pruel could no longer smell anything, and the copper-pointed slug did a wing-ding puree of the cerebrum taking the top of his head off like an eggshell surrendering to compressed air. Pow.

The brain stopped working at the beginning of the thought over whether he was going to see the flash of the powder down there at the other end of the barrel. He found out just before his brain was about to realize it. The answer was yes.

There were no more questions.

And no more need for the olfactory bulb.

CHAPTER SEVEN

Remo felt the skull fragment underneath his fin-
gerpads. Blood came heavy down the forehead
and as he wiped it off, he felt the familiar warm
wetness. He had been too slow. And now he had
paid for it. Much too slow.

He let the 30-30 rifle drop to the pavement in
disgust. He had reached the man just as he had
pulled the trigger and was too late. The man had
blown his own head off. He had been the pipe that
Remo might have traveled through to get to the
source. But now the man was dead and Remo had
nothing.

"That was fast," gasped Miss Viola Poombs.

"Slow," said Chiun. "He let that man kill himself. You cannot afford that. We needed that man
and we lost him."

"But he was shooting at everybody," said Viola.

"No," said Chiun. "He was shooting at me.
And at Remo."

"But he hit that poor, poor woman. He killed
that child."

"When one uses a machine for the first time,
one tests it."

"You mean he killed two people just to see if his gun worked? Oh, my god," cried Viola.

"No," said Chiun. "*He* was the machine. When you write your poem of the assassins, be sure to mention that the Master of Sinanju, foremost among assassins, decried the amateur at work. And he showed how cruel it was to use one. Innocents are killed when fools have weapons. The gun should never have been invented. We have always said that."

"What do you mean, he was the machine?"

"It was in his eyes," Chiun said. "Written there for all to see."

"How could you even see his eyes?" said Viola, still grabbing desperately to regain some form of pre-shock thinking. "I mean, how could you see it? There were shots and people getting killed and it was awful. How could you see his eyes?"

"When you, beautiful lady, walk into a room of other women, you can tell who wears what paint upon their face while to me it is a confusion of loveliness. But you know because you have seen before and have been trained to see. In such a manner are Remo and I trained to see. Death is not a confusing thing but a familiar thing. You might want to mention also when you write your story that not only is Sinanju effective but we have the most pleasant assassins that one can ever meet. If you don't count Remo." And Chiun folded his long fingernails and delicate hands back into his kimono on that pleasant spring afternoon in front of the new massive FBI building.

Inside, federal agents were phoning their personal lawyers to see if they were allowed to make an arrest concerning the killings below since technically the sidewalk might be city property, not federal property, and some local prosecutor might want to make a name for himself by prosecuting another federal servant. Increasingly in America, nobody ever got prosecuted for letting a criminal escape. The people were getting what they had been assured were civil liberties that would usher in a new golden age of love. Shootouts in what used to be their cities, while lawmen fearfully looked over their shoulders.

When the shots had first rung out, window shades were hastily drawn in the FBI building.

Viola Poombs looked to the building and no one came out. And then she saw something that made her retch.

Remo was drinking blood.

"What is wrong?" asked Chiun.

"He's drinking that man's blood," she said.

"No. He is touching his finger to it and smelling it. Blood is the window of health. In it you can smell, and therefore see, whatever is wrong with a person. Although he did not have to do that. Because in its gracious wisdom, Sinanju already knows the actions were those of a drugged man. He probably, before he killed himself, thought he had killed us."

"You can read minds too?"

"No," said Chiun. "It is really simple if you have seen it before. If you throw a pebble and hit a gong, and throw another pebble and hit a a gong, and throw another pebble and missed a gong, what would you do?"

"I'd throw another pebble at the gong I missed."

"Correct. And when the dead man shot at me and missed, he did not shoot again at me, but shot

102

at Remo, and when he missed, he did not shoot again at Remo, but at himself, to eliminate the link to those who used him. But he did not fire at us again because he thought he had hit us. When one hires Sinanju, you may write, what may seem expensive is really economy. For how expensive is a failed assassination? We will show you for your book."

"Aren't assassins supposed to be secret?"

"Amateurs need secrecy because they are refuse. The world suffers because of amateur murders who pretend to be assassins. Look at your two western wars, the first started by an amateur at Sarajevo, and the first leading to the second which will lead to the third."

"You mean the world wars?"

"Korea was not in them," said Chiun and this meant that since the most important country was not involved, he didn't care what Europeans and Japanese and Americans did to themselves. One had to have perspective. What those wars had done was to loose thousands of lunatics with weapons of vast destructiveness upon each other, instead of the neat, healthful, and useful, clean assassination that is done, buried and out of the way, with the body politic all the better off for the cleansing of nuisances.

Viola Poombs looked back toward Remo and saw the three bodies and the child so helpless and she became dizzy until the long fingernails of Chiun worked the nerves in her spine and she saw sunlight and the people clearly again. The Oriental had cleared away her fear-caused dizziness with a brief massage.

"We talk about seeing," said Chiun. "Now what is moving differently around here?"

Viola looked around. People were screaming. One had passed out in front of a small hydrant. A large crowd was forming. A car nearby slowly pulled out into the street, quite evenly and quite smoothly.

"I know this sounds crazy but that car is different."

"Exactly," said Chiun. "It does not respond to the hysteria around. You might point out in your book that an amateur assassin does not notice these things. Cheap help never notices these things. I know you are a craftsman and should not be told how to do your work but in your book you might want to describe this as 'The Master of Sinanju cast his glorious gaze upon the sea of milling whites, scurrying helpless in their confusion. "Lo," he cried. "Fear not for Sinanju is among you."' You can use your own words, of course," Chiun said helpfully.

Viola saw Remo take off after the car she had noticed. He didn't run like other men she had seen. Others pumped their legs. They strained and jammed. This was more of a float.

She did not see his lean figure start. Rather she knew he was running after he had begun to move. At first she thought he was going very quickly for someone who was running so slowly and then she realized that he wasn't running slowly at all. There was just such an economy of motion, it appeared slow.

Remo met the car like someone becoming glued to the side of it and then pop, bang, and out came a door and one man went crashing into a fire hydrant. The hydrant didn't move. The man moved a little. He let the blood flow out of the big hole in his chest that had met the hydrant. It had appeared as if he were shot out of the car by hydraulic compression.

"Wow," said Viola.

The car stopped. A thick-wristed hand beckoned to Viola and Chiun.

"Wow what?" asked Chiun. "Why are you excited?"

"It looked like he was shot out of that Buick Electra."

"What is a Buick Electric?"

"Electra. That car your friend just threw that guy out of."

"Oh," said Chiun. "Come. Let us go. He beckons."

"How did he do that?" asked Viola.

"He put out his hand and waved for us to come. It is a signal we use. Anyone can do it. Just wave your hand," said Chiun.

"No. Throw that guy out of the car so hard. How did he do that?"

"He threw," said Chiun, trying to pinpoint her wonder. When one properly did what one was taught and it was correct for the situation, one could hit almost any object with a person. Perhaps she was amazed that Remo had hit the American street water device so accurately. "If the car is moving, you have to lead the target so that you will hit it and not miss," Chiun said.

"No. The force of it. How'd he do that?"

"By listening to the wisdom of the House of Sinanju," said Chiun, who was still not altogether sure what Miss Poombs meant. Often people who lacked control of their bodies and their breathing were amazed by the simplest thing the human body could do when it did things properly.

Chiun guided Viola into the rear seat. A man with his hand on a .45 caliber revolver sat in the far corner of the rear seat. The gun lay on his lap. He had a small smile on his face. Very small. It was the sort of smile one gives when one realizes he has done something very stupid. In the case of the man with the .45 on his lap, the stupid thing was trying to fire the gun at the man with thick wrists who had invaded the car.

His life had ended mid-attempt. There was a small concavity above his left ear, just enough to compress the temporal lobe back into the hypothalamus and optic chiasma. Those were parts of the brain. The message the brain got when the temple stopped caving in was "All over. Stop work, fellas." It had been a very fast message. The heart had given two reflexive pumps, but since the vital organ of the brain had stopped, it stopped too.

The kidneys and liver, not getting blood from the heart to make them function, were preparing to shut down also. This general strike of the body was known as death.

"It's all right, Miss Poombs," said Chiun. "He won't bother you."

"He's dead," said Viola.

Remo, sitting with his arms over the front seat, next to a driver who was exercising an overwhelming call to be incredibly cooperative with the man who had emptied the car of all other living things, took offense at Miss Poombs' tone.

"He's not dead. He will live in the hearts of those who make stupid moves forever."

"What did he do that you killed him?" asked Miss Poombs. That man with the gun was dead.

106

Totally dead. Forever, unchangeably dead, and what did he do, other than be in a car that drove away from a killing scene at a controlled, smooth pace?

"Do?" asked Remo. "He did what will get you killed almost always, sweetie. He didn't think. His second biggest crime was not moving quickly enough with that gun. Stupid and slow are the two crimes in this world that are always punished."

Chiun pressed a reassuring hand on Viola Poombs' trembling arm.

"Miss Poombs, that man died because he offended our honor," said Chiun. He watched her face. It still looked as if someone had jammed two electrodes into her ears. She was terrified. She inched away from the body in the corner and her neck was very stiff as though if she did not keep it that way, she might look to her left where that was. Where *it* was. That thing. And Viola didn't want to look to her right either, because that was where the Oriental was who thought there was nothing wrong with any of this.

"Miss Poombs, he offended your honor violently. He has been killed in honor of the great artist who will write the story of Sinanju."

"I want to get out of here," cried Viola. "I want to go back to Poopsie. To hell with money for books on assassins."

"We killed him because he had bad thoughts in his head about the way the world should be run," said Chiun, trying something he thought would appeal to the white mind.

"Viola," said Remo coldly, "shut up. He's dead because he tried to kill me. This car was the connection to that man who killed the woman and child. Those deaths were ordered from this car. So were our deaths. They made a mistake. They weren't successful. They died because they failed to kill us. That's why they're dead."

"I like politics better. Nobody ever got hurt by taking off their clothes for an American congressman."

"Viola," said Remo, "you're in this thing. When it's over, you can leave."

Chiun tried to calm Miss Poombs but when the body fell forward, she buried her head in her hands and sobbed.

Remo talked to the driver. There were a few friendly questions. They were answered with great sincerity. And with no information. The driver had been hired that afternoon from Megargel's Rent-A-Car. And he was scared. Shitless. As he proved.

CHAPTER EIGHT

The first three times the President had sat in the White House, with television cameras peering in, to take telephone calls from the American public, the ratings had been pretty good. But the fourth and fifth times had been disasters. They had been outdrawn in New York by a rerun of *The Monte-fuscos* and in Las Vegas by the 914th showing of Howard Hughes' favorite movie.

A network executive explained it to a presidential aide. "Face up to it. In viewer interest, this phone bit ranks somewhere between watching grass grow and watching paint dry. Say about equal to watching water evaporate. So we're not going to televise any more of these things. Sorry you feel that way, old buddy. So's yours."

The presidential aide explained this to the President. "Jus' don't seem like no point in goin' on with it," he said.

"We'll do it," the President had said, without looking up from the foot-high stack of papers on his desk. Bureaucrats always seemed to complain about the massive amounts of paperwork connected with their jobs. But paperwork was information, and information sustained the presidency.

The country could survive a wrong, even a stupid, decision; it was harder to survive an ignorant, uninformed decision, because the latter all too often became administration policy. This was the first President who loved paperwork, because he was the first since Thomas Jefferson to understand the scientific method and the need for data.

"But sir?"

The President carefully put his yellow Number Two Excellent Pencil into a silver cup on his desk and looked at his aide.

"First, I take these phone calls to stay in touch with America, not for TV coverage. If I want the television people to get interested in me, all I've got to do is put on a tutu and practice ballet dancing on the west lawn. Just tape the program and maybe someday we'll find some use for it." He looked at the aide with a blank expression that did not contain a question, a request for confirmation, but only a demand for silence.

The aide nodded and smiled. "Good politics, sir."

The President picked up his pencil again and began to jot numbers into the margin of a report on overseas food distribution. "Good government," he said.

The aide looked crestfallen and chagrined as he walked to the door. He heard the President's voice and turned.

"*And* good politics," the President added with a large warm smile. After the aide left, the President allowed himself a sigh. The toughest part of any leader's job was always the personal relationships. Even men who had been with him for years still took disagreement for disapproval, still felt that if the President did not do what

110

they thought he should do, it somehow made them less worthy.

He thought that if he didn't have to spend so much time and energy stroking his staff, stroking the Congress, even stroking his own family, why . . . why he could read even more papers. He smiled grimly and went back to his work.

So it was that four nights later, he sat at a desk in another part of the building, punching buttons in the base of a telephone and talking to Americans who had called the White House to talk to their leader and had survived the screening of three separate White House staffers.

"A Mister Mandell, sir. One Two. With a question on energy."

The President punched the second button on the base of the telephone.

"Hello, Mister Mandell. This is the President. You wanted to talk about energy?"

"Yes. You're going to run out of it."

"Well, yes, sir, we all face that danger unless we reduce our . . ."

"No, Mr. President. Not we, you. *You're* going to run out of energy. On Saturday."

The death threat, if that's what it was, made him think. There was something in the voice that said this was no crank. The voice lacked zealous intensity, the high pitch that hate callers always had. This voice was matter of fact, laconic. It sounded like a control tower operator or a police radio car dispatcher.

The President made a note. "Fortyish. Touch of twang. Maybe Virginia."

"What do you mean, sir?"

"Remember Sun Valley, Utah? Your turn comes Saturday. You're going to die and I'm going to tell you where. On the steps of the Capitol. I warned you this would happen if you didn't pay."

The President waved his hand to one of his staffers to get off their own calls and pick this one up. He hoped they had enough cross-checking procedures on calls to trace where this call had come from.

"What do you mean, sir, by Sun Valley?" the President said.

"You know very well what I mean. That man thought he was protected too, and we killed him just to show he wasn't. We thought the lesson wouldn't be lost on you. But instead you brought in extra personnel. They can't help you, though. You're going to die."

"Suppose we offer to pay what you want?" the President asked. He caught the eye of his aide who was already talking into another telephone, putting the federal crime fighting apparatus in motion to go wherever that phone call was being made from and to collect the telephone caller.

"It's too late for that now, Mr. President," the phone caller said. "You're going to die. And I won't be at this location long enough for your people to get to me, so don't waste your time or mine. You might however leave a note for your successor. Tell him we do not like being ignored and when we call him—next Sunday after he's President—he had better not turn us down. Goodbye, Mr. President. Until Saturday."

The telephone clicked dead in the President's ear.

He replaced the telephone on the receiver and stood up behind his desk. He wore a light blue cardigan sweater with the sleeves pushed up past his ample farmer's wrists.

"I don't feel like taking any more of these calls," he said. The men near him moved forward. His closest aide was still leaning over his own telephone, his back to the President, talking.

The aide put the telephone down angrily and turned back to the President. He shook his head 'no.'

"Keep on it," the President said.

Before leaving the room, he whispered into the aide's ear. "Nothing to the press. Nothing at all. Not until I get a chance to think this through."

"Yes sir. Are you feelin' all right?"

"I'm fine. I'm fine. I've got to go upstairs now. I've got my own phone call to make."

Sylvester Montrofort hunched forward in the wheelchair behind his desk, ostensibly listening to Remo, but his eyes locked, as if by radar, on a point midway between the two foremost promontories of the Viola Poombs' anatomy.

He had started the meeting with the three strangers by sitting dead level with their eyes. But the overhang of the desk restricted his view of Viola's bosom and belly and legs and surreptitiously, inch by inch, he had raised his chair, until now he towered a foot over the rest of them, staring down at Viola.

She was busy taking notes. Like most people to whom writing is not a natural function, she accomplished it in bursts of enthusiasm, by fits and starts, and each start set off tiny movements in her chest, and gave Montrofort fits.

"This Pruel was one of yours," Remo said. "So what happened to him?"

"I don't know," said Montrofort, without changing the direction of his glance. "He had just come back from a mission in Africa. He was distraught, don't you know. Like a woodchuck who goes back to his hole and finds it filled with snakes. He wanted to resign. He said he had enough years of killing and worrying about killing."

"What did he have to do with killing?"

"Slow down," Viola said to Remo. She lifted her head to look toward him. "You're going too fast." Her breasts rose. Montrofort agreed. "Yes. Slow down. I've got plenty of time."

Remo shrugged. "What. Did. He. Have. To. Do. With. Killing? Got that?"

"Almost," said Viola.

"He was in the business of security. We provide security for people," Montrofort said. "Heads of state, wealthy men, men that somebody is always out there, planning to pick off like a year-old scab."

"Now *you're* going too fast," Viola said.

"Sorry, my dear." He paused to let her catch up, and waited till her eyes lifted and met his with a slight nod. "Also, Pruel had been in the Secret Service for many years dealing with presidential security. All our people have. That puts a lot of pressures on them. I guess the pressure finally got to him. You know how it is."

"He knows how it is," said Chiun. "He reacts very badly to pressure himself."

Remo looked disgusted. "And these two men in the car? They worked for you, too."

"Actually, they were on my payroll but they worked for Pruel. They were part of his personal staff. This here has got me as confused as a fly in

114

a cup of soup. I don't know why Pruel might have been trying to kill you. What reason? I don't know. And these other two, they must have been trying to help him. Don't ask me why. Maybe they just didn't like your looks. Maybe you frightened them, old buddy."

"Highly unlikely," said Chiun. "Look at him. Who could be frightened of that?"

"Hush," said Remo.

"Slower," said Viola. "I only got up to 'unlikely.' "

"I have it all in here," Montrofort said. He opened his desk drawer and brought out a small tape recorder. "When we're all done, why don't you stay and you can transcribe from the tape."

"Couldn't you just give me the tape?" she said.

"I'm sorry, dear. I can't do that. Company policy. But I'd be glad to help you copy it down if you wished."

"Well, maybe . . ."

"Sure," said Remo. "That's going to be good for you. And Chiun and I have other things to do."

"If you think it's all right," Viola said.

"Nothing could be righter," Remo said.

At the doorway, Remo stopped and turned to Montrofort who had returned his wheelchair to floor level and was moving around the side of the desk toward Viola.

"One thing, Mr. Montrofort. Did you know Ernest Walgreen?"

"One of our clients. Another ex-Secret Service man. We lost him. First client we ever lost." While he spoke he was staring at Viola's breasts and moving inexorably nearer and nearer to them. Suddenly he looked up at Remo. "Walgreen

115

was Pruel's case, too. Do you think all of this is tied up somehow?"

"Never can tell," Remo said.

Outside the forty-story glass-sided office building, Chiun said, "He lusts, that one."

"I feel kind of sorry for him," Remo said.

"You would."

CHAPTER NINE

"The President has been warned that he will be killed on Saturday." Smith's voice had sounded as if he were the telephone company's tape-recorded weather report, minus the fire and passion that precipitation probabilities carried with them.

"Where?" asked Remo.

"Outside the Capitol. He is supposed to address some rally of the young Students United against Oppression Overseas."

"Simple," said Remo. "Tell him to stay home."

"I already have. He refuses. He insists upon going to that rally."

"Screw him then," Remo said. "He's not as smart as I thought he was."

"I'd rather try to protect him," Smith said. "You don't have anything?"

"Don't have anything? I've got everything. I've got too much and none of it goes anywhere."

"Try it on me," Smith said. "Maybe the two of us might see something you overlooked by yourself."

"You're welcome to it," said Remo. "First, Walgreen. After Kennedy was killed, the Secret Service started paying off somebody who threatened to kill the next President. Walgreen was out of the service then but they recruited him to act as the bag man. So far, so good. Now this President, he won't pay. So our friendly little assassin kills off Walgreen. Very well, too. He put him in a safe hole and then he blew him away. You staying with me?"

"I'm with you," said Smith.

"Pay attention. I'm going to ask questions later," Remo said. "Now Walgreen tried to get protection. He went to a security agency called Paldor's. It's filled with old Secret Service hands. They couldn't protect him. Now this Paldor's. Yesterday, three of its guys tried to kill me."

"And me, too," said Chiun from across the room. "Do I count for nothing around here?"

"And Chiun," Remo said. "Now I would have said those guys who tried to kill me were the ones threatening the President, but—when'd you say the threat to him came?"

"I didn't say, but it was last night."

"Okay. It came after these three were dead. So they didn't have anything to do with it. And I don't know who does. Can't we just buy the bastards off?"

"The President asked about that," Smith said. "They said no."

"Then they're not in it just for the money. They've got something else in mind," Remo said.

"Right. It would seem so."

"Or maybe they're just loonies, and they're not playing with a full deck anymore," Remo suggested.

"That could be too."

"Who threatened the President?" Remo asked.

"A telephone call. Mid-southern voice. Forties. They traced the call to a rundown apartment in the east side of the city. Rent was paid three months in advance in cash. Nobody ever saw or remembers the tenant. The phone had been hooked up for two months but this was the first call apparently that had been made anywhere. They're trying to find somebody, either in the building or the phone company or somewhere, who might have seen the tenant, but no luck yet. And they've looked for prints, but they haven't found any."

"Tuesday, huh?"

"Yes. Two days to work."

"That's plenty of time," Remo said.

"You think you have an idea," said Smith.

"Yeah. But I can't talk about it now," Remo said.

After he had hung up, Remo told Chiun about the threat to the President.

"It is clear then what we must do," Chiun said.

"What's that?"

"We must tell this Viola Poombs that the President has rejected our advice so she can be sure to put it in her book. And then we must leave the country. No one can blame us for what will happen if we are not here and anyway he did not take our advice."

"Frankly, Chiun, I'd hoped we could find something better than just protecting our own reputations. Maybe like saving the President's life."

"If you insist upon trivializing everything, go ahead," Chiun said. "But important is important. The reputation of the House of Sinanju must be protected."

119

"Well, it doesn't matter," Remo said. "I've got a plan."

"Is this as good as your plan once to go look for Smith in Pittsburgh because you knew he was in Cincinnati or some name like that?"

"Even better than that one," Remo said.

"I can't wait to hear this wonderful plan."

"I can't tell you about it," said Remo.

"Why not?" asked Chiun.

"You'll laugh."

"How quickly you become wise."

When he was given the money, Osgood Harley had been given specific instructions. He was to go to 200 different stores. He was to buy 200 Kodak Instamatics and 400 packages of flashcubes. One camera and two packs of cubes in each store. The orders had been precise and specific and he had been warned about deviating from them.

But 200 stores? Really.

He had bought fourteen of them at fourteen different stores and carefully stashed them in his fourth-floor walkup apartment on North K Street. But at the Whelan's drugstore on the corner near his apartment, he got to thinking. Who would know? Or care?

"I'd like a dozen Instamatic cameras," he told the clerk.

"I beg your pardon."

"A dozen. Twelve. I'd like twelve Instamatic cameras," Harley said. He was five feet, eight inches tall with thin stringy hair that wasn't blond enough to look anything but dirty. The clerk noticed this as he looked up at the slack-jawed young man who was wearing four buttons.

One protested racism, police brutality, poverty; while three endorsed American Indians, the Irish Republican Army, and reopening of trade markets with Cuba.

"Twelve cameras. That's very expensive. Thinking of starting your own store?" the middle-aged clerk said with what he presumed to be a smile.

"I've got the money, don't worry about it," Harley said, peeling a roll of fifties from the front pocket of his white-streaked bleached jeans.

"I'm sure of that, sir," said the clerk. "Which model would you like?"

"Farrah Fawcett-Majors."

"I beg your pardon."

"The model I'd like. Farrah Fawcett-Majors."

"Oh, yes. Sure. Wouldn't we all?"

"The cheapest one," Harley said.

"Yes sir." The clerk turned the key locking the register and went into the back stockroom and brought down from a middle shelf a dozen Instamatics. None of his business, but who would buy a dozen Instamatics at once? Maybe the young man was a schoolteacher, and this was for a new class in photography starting up somewhere.

The bill with tax came to almost two hundred dollars. Harley started counting out fifties.

"Oh, shit. Flashcubes. I need two dozen packs of flashcubes," he said.

"Got 'em right here." The clerk tossed them into a bag. "And how about film, sir?"

"Film?" asked Harley.

"Yes. For the cameras."

"No. I don't need no film."

The clerk shrugged. The man might be crazy

121

but the fifty-dollar bills guaranteed enough sanity to do business with him.

He took five fifties from Harley and made change.

"Could I have your name, sir?"

"What for?"

"We often have specials here in the camera department. I can put you on our mailing list."

Harley thought a moment. "No. I don't want to leave my name."

"As you wish."

Harley walked out whistling with two large bags in his hands. The clerk watched him leave, noticing the slightly bowed legs, the run-down Hush Puppies, and practiced his powers of observation by remembering the four political buttons Osgood Harley wore on his short-sleeved plaid shirt.

A piece of cake, Harley thought. And he could save himself a lot of money in cab fares by buying in bulk. He wondered if there was a place nearby, a Kodak distribution center, where he could pick up the remaining 174 cameras he needed. Maybe he could have them delivered. Who would know? Or care?

Sylvester Montrofort was locked in his office, talking into the tape recorder secreted in the top right-hand drawer of his desk.

"Of course, by now that idiot is buying cameras in bulk. His is not the generation that can either follow instructions or do things the careful, correct way. Having him bungle will just make it that much easier for him to be picked up when the correct time comes. The fool."

Montrofort wanted to laugh but couldn't. He

tried to picture Osgood Harley in his mind's eye but all he could see was the formidable battlements of Viola Poombs, who was coming to dinner that night at his apartment.

CHAPTER TEN

"Hello, young fellow."

"How are you, Mr. President?" The speaker of
the House of Representatives was almost twenty
years older than the President and had been
fighting in political wars when the President was
still in high school. But he accepted the warmth
of the President's greeting with the eternal op-
timism of the professional politican, trying to
convince himself that it was not just *de rigueur*
warmth but an evidence of some deep-felt admi-
ration, affection, and trust. This was made more
difficult by the fact that he knew in his heart that
this President, like all the others, would peel off
his skin and tan it for *huaraches* if that was demanded by either the national interest or the
presidential whim.

"We've got to have lunch," the President said.

"My place or yours?" asked the speaker.

"I know I'm new around here but that's the
first time I've ever been mistaken for a nooner,"
the President said lightly. "Better make it mine.
The last time I ate over at the Capitol, there were
roaches in the building. I can't stand roaches."

"That was a long time ago, Mr. President. We haven't had roaches in two years."

"I'll take your word for it, youngster, but let's eat over here."

"What time, sir?"

"Make it one o'clock." The President paused. "And don't go telling any of those damned Boston Irish politicians where you'll be. We got us some heavy talking to do."

The speaker of the House listened through the soup and nodded through the salad but before the fried liver with bacon and onions arrived, he said, "You can't do it. That's all there goddam is to it, you can't do it."

The President raised a cautionary finger to his lips and the two men waited in awkward silence for the waiter to bring in their luncheon plates and clear away the soup and salad bowls.

When the private White House dining room was again empty but for them, the President said, "I've thought this through. I can't *not* do it."

"You're my President, goddam it. You can't go jeopardizing your life this way."

"Maybe. But I'm also the President of this country and if the President is going to be held hostage by the whims of some, I don't know what he is, lunatic, then this country better know about it, because it can't be governed any more and maybe we ought to find that out right away. I'm not going to spend four years hiding in here, skulking around, ducking under windowsills every time I walk past glass."

"That's a narrow view, sir," the speaker said hotly. "I've had one President shot out from under me and I've had another one blown away by his own stupidity. I'd rather have the President hiding and the presidency endure than have a brave President shot down. And on the Capitol steps? You can't do it. Case closed. *Roma locuta est.*"

"I always knew you yankees were gonna throw that damned Catholic altar boy stuff at me some day," the President said, his ample lips trying to smile. "Think about this, though. If I hide, who says the presidency endures? It's been hanging on by a thread since 1963. One President shot and another one forced to hide in the White House and another one thinking he was Louis the Fourteenth. So what've we got? A presidency that's a prison and a President who's a prisoner. Four years of my hiding and there won't be any presidency. The leader of this peckerheaded country may be a damned street mob, for all we know. I'm going and that's that." He hurried on quickly to silence any interruption. "Now the reason I called you here was this. I'm going to make sure the Vice President is at his desk on Saturday and doesn't leave this building for anything. And I don't want you on the Capitol steps with me. Or anybody else if you can swing it. You keep your guys inside."

"They're going to bitch that you're just trying to keep them off television. Another dirty political plot."

"Good. Let them bitch. Let them bitch like a constipated hound dog. And with luck they'll still be bitchin' at the end of the day, because everything's been a piece of cake, and maybe we can explain it to them."

"And if we can't . . . if . . ." The Speaker of the House could not bring himself to speak the word "assassination."

"If we can't, we'll know that we tried to do the right thing. Trust me. This is right."

After a long wait, the Speaker nodded glumly and began to toy with his liver. Maybe it was right. He had to trust and at least, he wasn't being asked to trust a President who thought he had to be a public macho symbol to the western world. This President's judgment would be cool and unemotional. But the Speaker still did not like the idea of a President walking into an assassination attempt, perhaps without any solid way of defending himself. He looked across the table at the man who sat in the nation's highest office. His face was wrinkled with the twisting gouge of the duties he handled every day; his skin was leathered like a man who had known what it was to make his living out of the inhospitable ground soil, whose own roots in America went back to the days when to survive meant to fight because it was a hostile land, and only the strong had endured. He looked at the President.

And he trusted him.

Remo didn't.

He moved through the darkened White House corridors like a silent wisp of smoke through a cigarette holder.

Secret Service men stood at every stairway and sat out of sight in alcoves at the intersection of each corridor in the living quarters of the President on the building's third floor. They were a palace guard, the first palace guard in history to ask questions first and to shoot later, Remo thought. But why not? America was a first in history too. The building he was in was an example of English Palladian architecture, designed by an Irishman, for the American chief of state. It was the story of the United States. It had been built by the best from everywhere and so, of all the nations in the world, it worked best. Not because its system was necessarily best, but because its people were the best to be found. That was why, no matter what America and its leaders tried to do, they could not export the American democratic system. It was a system designed by the best of the world, for the best of the world, and to expect cattle to understand it, much less emulate it, was asking too much of cattle.

Remo decided America had a much better, simpler policy for its relationships with the rest of the world.

"Screw 'em all and keep your powder dry," he mumbled.

Remo realized he had spoken aloud when a voice answered from behind him: "My powder's very dry. Don't test it."

He turned around slowly to confront a Secret Service agent. The man wore a gray suit with a tieless shirt. He had a .45 caliber automatic aimed at Remo's belly, held tight to his hip in safe position, where no sudden move of hand or foot could reach it before the weapon could be fired.

"Who are you? What are you doing here?"

Remo realized the man was new to the White House detail. Good procedure didn't call for on-the-spot interrogations. It called for the intruder to be removed from the dangerous area, and then questioned at length somewhere else.

"I'm looking for the Rose Guest Room," Remo said.

"Why?"

"I'm sleeping over tonight and I went to the bathroom but I got lost trying to get back. I'm the Dali Lama."

There was just a moment's hesitation, just a split second of confusion on the face of the agent, and Remo moved slowly to his right, then darted in quickly to his left. The automatic was out of the agent's hand, and Remo's right thumb and index finger were alongside the large carotid artery in the man's neck, squeezing just hard enough to cut off blood flow and sound. The man collapsed and Remo caught him in his arms, and carried him over to put him on the chair, underneath a large oval gilt mirror.

He put the man's automatic back in his shoulder holster. He had no more than five minutes and he would have to move quickly now.

He found the room he wanted and did what he had to do quickly, and then was back out in the corridor moving in the shadows to the President's bedroom. His thin body flowed through the corridors, drifting in and out of shadows, his body rhythms not those of a man walking or running, but randomly smooth, like the passage of air, and no more seen or noticed than the movement of air molecules.

Then Remo was in the presidential bedroom. The First Lady lay on her side, both hands under the pillow, snoring lightly. She wore a rhine-

129

stoned mask over her eyes to keep out the light from her husband's late-night in-bed reading. The President slept on his back, his hands folded over his bare chest, his body covered only by a sheet.

The President's hands moved up when he felt something drop lightly on his chest. Military service had given him the light sleeping habit, and he woke quickly, moved his hands and felt the object. He tried to determine what it was in the dark but couldn't. He reached for the light, but his hand was stopped by another hand before it could reach the switch.

"Those are the braces out of your daughter's mouth," Remo's voice said. "As easy as that was, that's how easy you go on Saturday."

The President's voice was close enough to being cool for Remo to be impressed.

"You're that Remo, aren't you?" the President said in a hushed whisper.

"Yeah. One and the same. Come to tell you that you're staying home Saturday."

"You haven't found out anything yet?" the President said.

"Just enough to convince me you're a damned fool if you think you're going to some open-air rally to stroke a lot of teeny-boppers when someone wants to put you down."

"That's where we differ, Remo. I'm going."

"You'll be a brave corpse," said Remo. "We warned you before. You're dead meat. You're still dead meat."

"That's an opinion," the President said. He lowered his voice as his wife's steady regulated snoring stopped for a second, then resumed.

130

"I can't stay hidden in this building for four years."

"Not for four years. Just Saturday."

"Sure. Just Saturday. Then Sunday. Then all of next week . . . next month . . . next year . . . forever. I'm going." The presidential voice was soft, but it had a stubborn intensity to it that made Remo feel like sighing.

"I could keep you here," Remo said.

"How?"

"I could break your leg."

"I'd go on crutches."

"I could do something to your voice box and make you silent for the next ninety-six hours."

"I'd go anyway and watch somebody else read my speech."

"You're the stubbornest damned cracker I ever met," Remo said.

"Are you finished threatening me?"

"I guess so. Unless I can think of something else to do to you."

"All right. I'm going. That's that. If you can't do anything about it, forget it. I'll take my chances."

"Aaah, you politicians make me sick." Remo was moving through the blackness of the room toward the door.

The President's voice followed him.

"I'm not really worried, Remo," he said.

"That proves one of two things. You're brave or stupid."

"No. Just confident."

"What have you got to be confident about?" Remo said, as he paused with his hand on the doorknob.

"You," the President said. "You'll work something out. I trust you."

"Crap. I don't need that," Remo said. "Don't lose those braces. Dentists aren't cheap for kids with dead fathers."

CHAPTER ELEVEN

Actually, cripples didn't turn her on, but Viola Poombs was willing to sacrifice herself for her art.

So she dressed in a light blue wool sweater she had bought expressly because it would shrink to non-fit, and a tight white linen skirt that squeezed her buttocks like a pair of loving hands.

She had no intention of taking the clothes off, not that night, not for Sylvester Montrofort. Lookies, but no feelies. Maybe even a brush-touchie, but definitely no feelies.

She was admitted to Montrofort's penthouse apartment by a butler in a swallowtail coat, who took her light white shawl and managed to restrict his expression of distaste at her clothing to a quarter-inch lift of only one eyebrow.

When he led her into the dining room, Montrofort was already sitting in his wheelchair at the far side of an oak table, laden with shimmering crystal glasses and polished dinnerware and golden vermeil.

"Miss Poombs, sir," the butler announced as he escorted Viola into the high-ceilinged room, il-

luminated only by real candles in real candela-
bras placed about the room.

When Montrofort saw her, his eyes widened.
He rolled his wheelchair back out from between
the legs of the small dining table and like a de-
mented crab rolled around the table toward her
at high speed. The butler was already pulling her
chair away from the table. Montrofort slapped
the man's wrist lightly.

"I'll do that," he said.

Viola stood alongside the chair as Montrofort
pulled it away from the table. She moved over to
sit down, but as she did, the right rear leg of the
chair caught in the spokes of the right wheel of
Montrofort's wheelchair. Viola sat down, but
caught only the edge of the chair, threatening to
tip it forward.

She reached down to pull the chair under herself. The chair wouldn't move. She gave it a yank.
The yank pulled the chair forward. It also pulled
forward Montrofort's wheelchair because the
brakes were off. The back of her chair pushed
forward by the free-rolling Montrofort smashed
against her backside with enough force to slam
her face forward onto the table. Her head hit the
dinner plate. Two crystal glasses fell over and
shattered.

The wind was knocked from Viola's lungs as
the edge of the table dug deep into her belly. She
lay with her head on the plate, gasping for air.

"How nice to see you, my dear," said Montrofort. He was still struggling surreptitiously to
free Viola's chair leg from his wheel.

He finally wrenched it loose with a giant tug of
his muscular arms. Just at that moment, Viola
caught her breath and straightened up. The back

134

of the chair thrust ceilingward missed rapping Viola at the base of the skull by only a fraction of an inch.

Viola was standing now and Montrofort held her chair in his hands at eye level.

"Shit," he hissed under his breath. "Shall we try again, my dear?" he asked in a normal voice.

He rolled himself back a foot, placed Viola's chair on the floor, all four legs planted solidly, and motioned for Viola to sit down. Two feet from the table.

"Comfortable, child?" Montrofort asked.

"Yes. Very," said Viola. She stood up and leaned over to get a glass of water from the table, then sat back down on the chair. Montrofort stared at her buttocks as she moved. The butler hovered nearby, uncertain whether to come forward to help or not. He now moved into position to remove the shattered Waterford crystal from the table.

"Not now, Raymond," Montrofort said. "Just bring the wine."

Montrofort left Viola sitting in her chair, two feet from the table, and wheeled himself around to its other side.

He took up his dining position facing Viola, who still sat two feet from the table. Montrofort wore a powder blue foulard scarf around the open neck of his midnight blue velvet smoking jacket. He touched it and smiled. "We're color coordinated," he said.

Viola looked blank. "My tie and your sweater," he said. "Color coordinated."

"You'll have to talk louder," Viola said. "I'm so far away I can't hear you."

Montrofort let out an animal growl. He

reached both arms under the full table and lifted it six inches off the ground, then hunched his body forward to start his wheelchair rolling. It stopped with the edge of the table four inches from Viola's lovely belly and he carefully set the table down on the floor. And on Viola's right foot. She screamed and pulled her foot out from under the table leg.

"Are you all right?" Montrofort asked.

"I'm fine. I'm fine," she said with a smile. "It's really a nice table. I'm glad to be sitting here."

Montrofort wheeled himself into position at his end of the table, put his elbows on the table, his face in his hands, and smiled his rich broad smile at the woman. "I'm really pleased that you could come," he said.

He stared at her bosom. Viola noticed the stare and took her hands from the table in front of her, so her chest could be stared at with nothing in the way to impede the stare. She pressed her shoulders against the back of the chair, imagining that she was trying to make her shoulder-blades touch.

Montrofort's eyes widened. "Where is that butler with that wine?" he growled.

Viola imitated a yawn and stretched her arms over her head. Her breasts rose under the thin blue sweater. The itchy fabric felt good against her bare skin.

Montrofort's eyes did not leave her. His mouth was working again, but nothing came out.

"You look lovely tonight, my dear. Especially lovely."

"Do you know anything about residuals on a TV adaptation of a book?" Viola asked.

Raymond returned with a bottle of wine, the

first step in Montrofort's elegant and pure seduction plan. He was going to pour as much wine in Viola Poombs as it took to get her loaded, and then he was going to screw her eyes out.

"I'll ring when I want you again, Raymond," Montrofort said. He lifted the glass that Raymond had filled and held it up toward the candle-lit chandelier over the table.

"A Vouvray *pétillant*," he explained. "Very rare. Very exquisite. Like you. Shall I make the toast?"

Viola shrugged. She had already drunk half her glass of wine. She lowered it. "No, I'll make the toast."

She poured more of the $31-a-bottle wine into her goblet. Some spilled out onto the table. She hoisted the glass over her head.

"To money," she said.

"To us," Montrofort corrected blandly.

"To money and us," said Viola, then drained the glass of wine in one crazed gulp. "Pour me some more of that, will you?"

"Certainly, my dear. I did not fully share in your toast to money because I have all the money I shall ever need."

Viola's eyes rose from the table to meet Montrofort's. All the money he wanted. "*All* the money you want?" she said.

"All and more," said Montrofort, handing her back her wine glass, filled again.

He smiled at her. He really did have a nice smile, Viola thought. Nice teeth. He probably had had a good dentist. A good team of dentists working on his mouth. When one had *all* the money he could want, all and more, well, he could afford any kind of teeth he wanted. It was good for crippled dwarfs to have good teeth. People who liked teeth might be attracted to them. Viola, now, had always had a warm spot in her heart for people with good teeth.

"I love your good teeth," she said, swilling and spilling.

"Thank you, my dear. All my own. Never a cavity in my life."

Maybe he was cheap. If he had all the money he ever wanted, all and more, why didn't he spend some money on his teeth?

"Why not?" Viola asked. She pushed forward the wine glass for a refill.

"Why not what?"

"Why didn't you spend something on them?"

Montrofort tried to chuckle casually. Maybe she was crazy. "Your job with the Congress must be very interesting," he said. He handed her glass forward.

"How much did this wine cost?" asked Viola.

"Who cares about money?" said Montrofort. "Whatever it cost, it was a small price to bring you pleasure. Who thinks about money?"

"People who are too cheap to have their teeth fixed right," yelled Viola. She slammed her Waterford goblet on the table for emphasis. The stem snapped smartly, an inch up from the base. She held the rest of the wineglass as if it were a dixie cup, her hand around the fat bowl, and slurped down her wine. When she was done, she threw the goblet toward the fireplace. She missed.

"We were talking about your job with the Congress," Montrofort said. He looked around for another glass for Viola, but three had already been broken. The only one left was his. He filled it and handed it over.

"It's a job," Viola said. "The massage parlor I worked in, now that was interesting."

"You worked in a massage parlor? How droll."

"Yeah," Viola said, peeking out from around her uplifted wineglass. "Three years. That's where I met . . . whoops, no names."

"I understand, dear. I certainly do. From a massage parlor to Congress. How interesting."

"Yeah. The money was better in the massage parlor. Until now, anyway. With this book I'm gonna write. More of that wine, okay?"

"Your book should be very interesting." Montrofort upended the bottle over Viola's glass, filling it halfway.

Viola took the glass. "Yeah. About ashash . . . assash . . . about killings and like that."

"Oh yes. Assassinations."

"You're going to help me, aren't you?" Viola asked.

"Day and night. Weekdays and weekends. We can go visit the scenes of the great assassinations of history. Just you and me."

"Better bring somebody to wheel you around too. I don't wheel any too good," Viola said.

"Of course, my dear," said Montrofort.

"I need you to help me with my book, 'cause I don't write too good, and you talk like you could really write and all, and besides you know about things."

"Not only will I help you with the book, but when you make your million I'll help you manage your new-found wealth, if you wish."

"You don't have to do that," Viola said. "I work for Congress. I know all about Swish . . . Swish . . . Shwiss bank accounts."

"That's like the kindergarten, however, of

money hiding. To really eliminate all chance of being traced, you must wash your funds through Switzerland and then through more accounts in other friendly nations. African nations are particularly good because they make up their banking regulations to fit the customer and for five dollars you can buy all the treasury secretaries on the continent."

"Right. I see. We'll worry about that later," Viola said.

"Very wise. First the book, then the money," said Montrofort. Viola's head was nodding. Her eyelids drooped. It was the time to make his move.

"Why don't we go into my studio to discuss this further?" he said. "We can allocate responsibilities that each of us should have to insure a good book."

"Right," said Viola. "Lead the way." She yelled as if leading a charge of the cavalry. "Okay, everybody. Roll on out. You get it? Roll on out. Get it?"

"Yes, my dear. Follow me."

Montrofort rolled back from the table and toward a side door leading from the dining room. He opened the sliding door and turned to let Viola through first. She was not with him. She was still at the table, her head on her plate, the plate partially filled with wine from her overturned goblet, sleeping gently.

Montrofort rolled back to her side. She breathed deeply and steadily.

Cautiously he extended an index finger and touched one of Viola's breasts which hung threateningly over the floor.

"Unnh, uhnnh," Viola mumbled, her eyes still closed. "No feelies. Looksies."

"Please," said Montrofort to the sleeping woman.

"Only brush-touchies. No feelies. My lash word on the shubject. Now don't get fresh and make me have to wheel you into the fireplace."

"No, my dear," said Montrofort. He rolled to the dining room's main door, opened it, and summoned Raymond with an imperial crook of his finger.

The butler stepped forward hurriedly.

"Get her out of here, Raymond," Montrofort said.

"Shall I call her a cab?"

"No. Just put her on the curb," Montrofort said. "I'm going to bed."

A laughing stock, was he? He would see who would be laughing on Saturday. And he knew the answer.

No one in the country but him.

CHAPTER TWELVE

The sky's black was diluting into a deep gray when Remo came back to the hotel room. Chiun was sitting in the corner of the room on a fiber mat, watching the door.

"How did your wonderful idea work?" he asked as Remo came in through the unlocked door.

"I don't want to talk about it," Remo said.

"The man is an idiot."

"What man?"

"What man? The man you were talking to. The emperor with the funny teeth."

"How did you know I went to see him?"

"Do I know you, Remo? After all these years, don't you think I know what foolishness will strike your fancy?"

"He wouldn't go along. He's going to appear on Saturday."

"That's why he is an idiot. Only an idiot goes blithely rushing forward into danger, whose dimensions he knows not. Really, Remo, I don't know how this country has lasted long enough to have a bicenental celebration."

"Bicentennial," said Remo.

"Yes. And being run by idiots all that time. Americans always act as if they are protected by God. They drive those awful belching machines at each other. They poison each other with what they call food. There is a smokehouse in Sinanju where we smoke codfish, and it smells better than the air here. Despite that, you have lasted for a bicenental celebration. Maybe God does protect you idiots."

"Then maybe he'll protect the President."

"I hope so. Although how God can tell one of you idiots from another is beyond me. Since you all look alike."

"Actually, what the President said was that he had total faith in the Master of Sinanju. That he knew he was in the finest, strongest hands in the world."

"Hands, no matter how fine or strong, work only if they have something to clutch."

"He said he thought you would protect him."

"Impossible."

"He said nothing could stop you," Remo said.

"Except that which we know nothing of."

"He said if he survived this, he was going to take a commercial on television and tell everybody that the House of Sinanju was responsible for his protection."

Chiun unfolded his arms and let them drop to his sides. "He said that?"

"That's exactly what he said. I remember his exact words. He said, 'If I survive this, I'm going to go on television and say that I owe it all to the bravest, most wonderful, awe-inspiring, magnificent . . .'"

"Enough. He was clearly talking about me."

143

"Right," said Remo. "At last, you're going to get all the credit you deserve."

"I take it back. That man is not an idiot. He is just malicious."

"He just has faith in you, is all," Remo said.

"As soon as I heard him talk funny, I should have known. He cannot be trusted."

"Why are you all bent out of shape? Over a compliment?"

"Because if this man of many teeth goes on television and says that we are in charge..."

"I'm glad it's 'we' now," said Remo.

"When he says we are in charge of his protection and then if anything happens to him, what then becomes of the good name of Sinanju? Oh, the perfidy of that man."

"I guess we'll just have to save him," Remo said.

Chiun nodded glumly. "He is from Georgia, isn't he?"

"That's right."

"Stalin was from Georgia."

"That's a different Georgia. That's in Russia," Remo said.

"It doesn't matter. All Georgians are alike, no matter where they are from. Stalin was worthless too. Millions dead and no work for us. I was never so happy as when that man was killed by his own secret police."

"Well, buck up. You're working for a Georgian this time, and you've got plenty of work. You've got to help me save the President."

Chiun nodded. The first rays of sunlight were entering the room, and through the translucent pink curtain, the sun cut jagged lines of light across the angular yellow face.

144

Chiun looked toward the light, and with his back turned to Remo, said softly, "A Hole."

"What?"

"Do you remember nothing? The Hole. They are going to attack him and force him into The Hole for the real attack. We have to find out how."

"How do you know they'll do that?"

"Killers come and killers go, but all they have ever known or been or could hope to be, has come from the wisdom of Sinanju. I know they will do that because they seem to be less inept than the usual level of murderers you have in this country. Therefore they emulate Sinanju and that is the way I would do it."

"All right," Remo said. "We'll have to find The Hole."

Across the city, Sylvester Montrofort was wheeling his way down the hallway to his private office in Paldor Services Inc. He pressed a button on the right arm of his wheelchair and the sliding door to his office opened in front of him. There was already a man in the office. He was standing at the floor-to-ceiling windows, looking out through the brown-tinted glass at Washington, D.C., below. He was a tall man with hair so black it was almost blue. He was over six feet tall, and his suit was broad at the shoulder and nipped in at a narrow waist, and tailored so well that it was apparent that the suitmaker knew his only function was to wrap something well-fitting around a work of art that nature had already created.

Montrofort hated the man. He hated him more when the man turned at the sound of the opening door, and smiled at Montrofort with just as many perfect teeth as the dwarf had. The man had a healthy tanned face, masculine but not leathery. His eyes sparked with the kind of vitality that informed the world he saw humor and mirth where no one else could. His hands as he raised them toward Montrofort in a greeting were long and delicate and manicured, and had been known, upon necessary occasions, to drive an icepick through an enemy's temple.

Benson Dilkes was an assassin and his awesome skills had helped make Paldor the success it was in the international world of protection for money. None of the Paldor salesmen ever knew it, but the reason they were received so warmly in the emerging nations by the presidents-for-life and the emperors-for-life and the rulers-insurmountable-forever was that Dilkes had been in the countries only days before, mounting an assassination attempt that looked like the real thing, but missing by a hair. He prepared the field from which Paldor's salesmen harvested very rich contracts.

And on those rare occasions when a foreign leader decided he did not need protection, no matter how close the recent assassination attempt had been, Dilkes usually showed him he was wrong. And generally, the ruler's successor was smarter. And hired Paldor.

"Sylvester, how are you?" Dilkes said. He came forward to take Montrofort's hands in his. His voice had a raspy Virginia twang.

Montrofort ignored him and wheeled behind his desk. "Just the same as I was the last time I saw you two days ago," he said curtly.

Dilkes smiled, his even white teeth a badge of

beauty in his bronzed face. "Even two days without seeing you seems like an eternity."

"Can that bullshit, me bucko. You know that Pruel failed yesterday?"

"So I read in this morning's papers. Unfortunate. I think, if you'll remember, I volunteered to do the job for you myself."

"And if you'll remember I told you that I want this to be extra careful. I don't want no shirttails hanging out at all. Your job is that dipshit revolutionary, Harley. How is he doing?"

Before he answered, Dilkes came around and sprawled in one of the three chairs facing Montrofort's desk.

He bridged his fingers in front of his face. "Just as we expected," he said. "He tired quickly of buying the cameras individually and is now buying them in bulk, showing off his rolls of cash, and generally making himself most memorable for the investigation that will eventually come."

Montrofort nodded, his eyes riveted to Dilkes' face, cursing the man's handsomeness.

"I have to tell you, Sylvester, though. I still don't know why you're going through with this. They offered to reinstate the payments."

"I'm going through with it because I'm tired of being pushed around. I'm not a baby carriage."

"Who's pushing you around? Paying tribute is hardly abusive behavior," said Dilkes.

"Look. They paid. Then they stopped paying. If I let them get away with that, they'll stop paying sometime in the future again. They've got to know that we mean business, business, business. That's it."

Dilkes shrugged and then nodded. Of course, it had nothing to do with meaning business. It had to do with Sylvester Montrofort being a dwarf cripple and finally deciding to prove that, no matter what his body looked like, he was a man to reckon with. Reason had as much chance of stopping him as argument had of reversing the tide.

Dilkes pulled a hard plastic casino chip from his right jacket pocket and began rolling it across the tops of his fingers. "Of course, by now the President will have ordered Congress to stay out of the way," he said.

"More likely, just the leaders. Now if they're able to impose discipline, we'll have our congressmen just inside the Capitol entrance, waiting." Montrofort smiled for the first time that day, and fluttered his hands skyward in an imitation of a bird flying away.

"The surest trap is the one you set in the path of a man running to avoid a trip," Dilkes said.

"More of your eastern wisdom?" Montrofort said. His voice sneered.

"You should read more of it, Sylvester. You won't find it in libraries, but if you know where to look there is a body of literature out there that tells all of us, in this strange business, all we ever need to know."

"I believe in technology, baby. Give me that ology every time," said Montrofort. He was feeling better now, and he raised the level of the platform behind his desk so he was six inches higher than Dilkes.

"And I believe in Sinanju," Dilkes said.

Montrofort remembered something. He squinted at Dilkes.

"What'd you say?"

"I believe in Sinanju."

"And what's Sinanju?"

"An ancient order of assassins," Dilkes said. "Creators of the martial arts. Invisible in combat. Through the ages of history, they have been involved in every court, in every palace, in every empire. There's an old saying: 'When the House of Sinanju is still, the world is in danger. But when the House of Sinanju moves, the world continues only by sufferance.'"

"These are Koreans, aren't they?" asked Montrofort. He smiled slightly as he watched the cool, impeccable, unflappable Dilkes continue to roll the casino chip across the back of his fingers.

"*Were* Koreans. The last anyone heard is that there is only one Master left in the House. An aged, frail man who if he still lives must be retired. None know of him till this day. What's wrong, Sylvester? You looked as if you've swallowed a frog."

"Not know of him may be accurate," said Montrofort slowly. "But not till this day. Rather, yesterday. That Master's name is Chiun, he is eighty years old if he is a minute, and yesterday he was sitting on that very chair you now occupy."

The casino chip dropped to the carpeted floor. Dilkes jumped to his feet as if he had just been told his chair had been wired to the Smoke Rise generating station.

"He was here?"

"Yes. He was here."

"What did he do? What did he say?"

"He said that America was decadent because it did not love assassins. He said that American television was decadent because it had destroyed its only pure art form. He said that white and black and most yellows were decadent because they

149

were inferior races. And he told me that he wished he had met me when I was young, because he could have prevented me from being this way but now it was too late to do anything. That's what he said."

"But why? Why was he here?"

"Very simple. He is defending the President of the United States against assassin or assassins unknown." Montrofort smiled. Dilkes didn't.

"I'll tell you another thing, too, Dilkes. He was one of the guys Pruel was supposed to blow away yesterday."

"You tried to kill the Master of Sinanju?" said Dilkes.

"Yep. And I think I'll try again."

"Now you know why Pruel failed." Dilkes paused and looked behind him as if fearing something or someone had come in the door. "Sylvester, you and I have been friends and partners for a long time."

"That's right."

"It ends now. You can count me out."

"Why? All this over an eighty-year-old Korean?"

"I may be the greatest assassin in the western world . . ."

"You are," Montrofort interrupted.

"But compared to the Master of Sinanju I am a kazoo player."

"He is very old," said Montrofort. He was enjoying this. It was pleasant to watch the cool Dilkes panic. There were actually beads of sweat on the forehead of the big man. "Very old," Montrofort repeated.

"And I want to be. I am going back to Africa."

"When?" said Montrofort.

"An hour ago. Do what you're going to do yourself. Goodbye, Sylvester."

Dilkes did not wait for an answer. He stepped on the pressure-sensitive pad in front of the door and it slid open. It shut behind him just as the inkwell thrown by Montrofort hit the door. "Coward. Emotional cripple. Coward. Fraidy-cat," Montrofort screamed at the door, his voice as loud as it could be, knowing it would carry through the door, and Dilkes would hear him.

"You're a pussycat, not a man!" he screamed. "A coward! A lily-livered baby!" yelled Montro-fort.

And he smiled all the while.

CHAPTER THIRTEEN

"This is it," said Remo, waving his hand toward the cast-iron dome high overhead inside the main entrance to the Capitol.

"This is where the Constitution is kept?" Chiun asked.

"I don't know. I guess so."

"I want to see it," Chiun said.

"Why?"

"Do not patronize me, Remo," said Chiun. "For years, I have known what we do. How we work outside the Constitution so everybody else can live inside the Constitution. I would see this Constitution so I may know for myself what it is we are doing and if it is worthwhile."

"It pays the gold tribute every year to your village."

"My honor and sense of personal worth are beyond price. You would not understand this, Remo, being both American and white, but some are like that. I am one of them. We value our honor beyond any amount of riches."

"Since when?" asked Remo. "You'd work as an enforcer for a Chinese laundry if the price was right." He was looking past Chiun at a group of men standing off in a corner of the huge entrance hall.

"Oh, no. Oh, no," Chiun said. "And why are you looking at those fat men who drink too much?"

"I thought I recognized them," Remo said. "Politicians I think they are. Maybe congressmen."

"Them I would speak to," Chiun said. He walked away from Remo.

The Speaker of the House was the first to see the little yellow man approaching.

"Mum, men," he said and turned, smiling, toward Chiun, who approached, unsmiling, like a teacher on his way to confront an amphitheater of parents whose children had been left back.

"Are you a congressman?"

"That's right, sir. Can I help you?"

"A long time ago I was very angry with you because you put on the Gatewater show of all you fat men talking and you took off my television shows. But now the shows are no good anymore, anyway, because they are decadent, so I don't care that they are off. Where is the Constitution?"

"The Constitution?"

"Yes. You have heard of it. It is the document I am supposed to be working to protect, so that all of you can be happy as clams, while I do nothing but work, work, work on your behalf. The Constitution."

The Speaker of the House shrugged. "Damned if I know, sir. Neil? Tom? You know where the Constitution is?"

"Library of Congress, I think," said Neil. He had a thin pinched face that was unhealthily red-blotched. Thinning gray hair swirled around his head in windblown swoops.

153

"Maybe the national archives," said the congressman named Tom. He had a face that was strong and open, an invitation to trust. It looked as if it had been carved from a healthy potato.

"You gentlemen work here?" Chiun said.

"We are congressmen, sir. Glad to meet you," said Neil extending his hand.

Chiun ignored the hand. "And you work for the Constitution and you don't know where it's kept?"

"I work for my constituents," said Neil.

"I work for my family," said Tom.

"I work for my country," said the speaker.

"I used to work for Colgate, though," said Neil brightly.

"That's nothing," said Tom. "I used to deliver newspapers on cold winter mornings."

"Lunatics," said Chiun. "All lunatics." He walked back to Remo. "Let us leave this asylum."

"You said we've got to find The Hole where the President is vulnerable. He'll be talking on the front steps. Now where's The Hole?"

Chiun was not listening. "This is a strange building," he said.

"Why?"

"It is very clean."

"It costs enough. It ought to be clean," Remo said.

"No, it is cleaner than that. There has never been a castle that was not infested. But this one is not."

"How can you tell that? There could be little buggies everywhere, just peeking out at you, waiting for night time so they can come out and dance."

"Dance on your own face," said Chiun. "There are none here and that is very unusual in a castle."

"This isn't a castle, Chiun. It isn't a palace. This is a democracy. Maybe cockroaches are monarchists."

"This country is run by one man?" Chiun asked.

"Kind of."

"And he has a secret organization that we are part of?"

"Right."

"And we kill his enemies whenever we can?"

Remo shrugged at the onrushing inevitable.

"Then this country is like any other," Chiun said. "Except here they take longer to do things. The difference between this place and an absolute monarchy is that the absolute monarchy is more efficient."

"If they were so efficient, why couldn't they do anything about the cockroaches in the castles?" asked Remo.

"Remo, sometimes you are terribly stupid."

"Hah. Why?"

"Listen to your nasal honking. 'Hah.' You would think I never taught you to speak, to listen to you."

"Don't correct my speech. Tell me about cockroaches."

"Cockroaches are always with us. They abound. In the pyramids, in the storied temples of Solomon, in the castles of the French Louis, they abound."

"And we don't have them here?"

"Of course, there are none here. Do you hear them?"

"No," Remo admitted.

"Well?"

"You mean you can hear cockroaches?" Remo asked.

"I refuse to believe that a Master of Sinanju has been reduced to this," Chiun said. "Standing here in the hallowed halls of your watchamacall-it..."

"Capitol. The Congress building."

"Yes. That. That I am standing here in these hallowed halls talking about cockroaches to someone no better than a cockroach himself. My ancestors will judge me harshly for having let Sinanju be dragged down into the mud like this."

"If I'm a cockroach, and we're co-equal partners, what does that make you?"

"A trainer of cockroaches. Oh, woe is Sinanju."

Osgood Harley scratched himself awake, trying to dig his stubby bitten fingernails into his pale white belly. The flesh was wrinkled from the tight waistband of the jeans he had slept in. He would pay dearly for having drunk two bottles of wine and passing out in his clothes, because sleeping in his clothes made his groin sweat, and an unpowdered sweaty groin gave him jock itch, the most persistent and incurable of all mankind's diseases.

There hadn't been jock itch in the old days. And there hadn't been drinking alone in a shabby walkup.

There had been action. Committees to protest this or that, and coalitions to promote this or that, and there had been television coverage, and newspaper interviews, and there had been a lot of money, and chicks. Oh, had there been chicks, and he had slept his way from bed to bed from Los Angeles to New York, from Boston to Selma.

And then the revolutionary fervor had vanished. The Vietnam war had pumped billions of dollars into America's economy. Almost everybody was working and every paycheck was fat and the money drifted down from the workers to their children, giving them the freedom to spend their time protesting—even against the war which made the protests possible. But as the war dried up, the economy dried up, and would-be revolutionaries found out it wasn't so much fun when there wasn't a check in the mailbox from Daddy, and so they cut their hair and swapped their sandals for shoes and went to college to study accounting or law, and with luck, wound up with a Wall Street firm and a steady paycheck.

The "leaders" of the revolution got caught in the switches. Suddenly, the money to support their free-living style had dried up. Some of them adjusted quickly. They peddled drugs; they joined religious movements; used to the fast buck, they went wherever they could find the fast buck.

Osgood Harley didn't, because unlike the majority of others, he really believed in a revolution, really wanted the overthrow of capitalist society. And so when the tall man with the black hair and the manicured nails and the beautiful even teeth had looked him up and offered him five thousand dollars if he would participate in a plan to embarrass the new American President, Harley gobbled at the chance.

Of course, it could have been better. Harley could have worked in public—with mimeographed press releases, and headquarters, and picketers, and sign-carriers—the way he had always worked in the past. But this time, he was told firmly "no." Any publicity and Harley could forget the five thousand dollars. With forty-nine cents in his pocket and a hole in the bottom of his Adidas sneakers, Harley found the choice easy. He would be as silent as smoke.

Even if the instructions about buying 200 cameras in 200 stores were stupid.

Harley had just stopped scratching when the doorbell rang. The young man standing in the hall wore a peaked cap with Jensen's Delivery Service embroidered across the front. In his arms he held a large cardboard carton.

"Mr. Harley?"

"One and the same."

"I've got some cameras here for you."

"Thirty-six to be exact. Come on in." He held the door back and let the younger man enter.

"Want them any special place?"

"Not there. Over there near the closet. That's where I've got the rest of them."

"Rest of them? You've got more?"

"Sure. Doesn't everybody?" Harley said casually.

"You must be opening a store," the youth said as he carefully set the box on the floor.

"Naah. Actually I'm a secret agent for the CIA and this is my newest mission." He grinned the kind of grin designed to impart the feeling that there was more truth than humor in what he had just said. The young man looked at his face with a reciprocal smile, but with narrowed eyes, as if memorizing Harley's face in case they asked questions later.

"There you go," he said.

"Good. Thanks. You saved me a lot of trouble."

Harley took a roll of bills from his pocket and flashed the wad of fifties, before digging down into the center of it to find a ten-dollar bill.

"Here. For you. Thanks again."

"Okay, Mr. Harley. Really appreciate it."

After the delivery boy left, Harley gave the big carton of Instamatics, purchased at individual list price from a large camera store in the heart of the city, a healthy kick. He was beginning to think this was all kind of stupid. So he had his 200 cameras. So what? Wait for more instructions.

The more he thought about it, the more stupid it became. So he gave the carton another kick. The sound was answered, as if by a sportive echo, by the ringing of the doorbell.

Harley recoiled slightly before going to the door. It was the delivery boy again.

"I found this downstairs on the hall radiator. It's got your name on it." He handed forward a plain white envelope with "Osgood Harley" neatly lettered on it.

"Thanks, kid," Harley said.

After the boy left, Harley opened the envelope. There was a simple hand-printed note inside: *Bring pencil and paper to the telephone booth at 16th and K Streets at 2:10 P.M. exactly.*

The note was unsigned.

Harley got to the telephone booth at 2:12 P.M., delayed because he had to stop and have an Italian ice. The telephone did not ring until 2:15 P.M.

"Hello, Harley here," said Harley when he picked up the telephone.

"Clever," said the caller.

"I mean, hello," said Harley, who suspected

from the sarcasm that he had made a mistake but couldn't be sure what it was.

"Do you have pencil and paper?"

"Right here," Harley said.

"Since you have already obtained the cameras, it is time to move on. You need one dozen cap pistols, the kind children use. Write it down. One dozen cap pistols. Get good ones. The loudest you can get. Don't, however, be an idiot and test them in the store.

"Have you got that?"

"Got it," Harley said. "A dozen cap pistols. Loud ones."

"Before you repeat anything else, please close the door of the telephone booth," the caller said. He waited until Harley pulled the door click-closed.

"All right. You also need four cassette tape players. Be sure they are battery operated and run at $1\frac{7}{8}$ inches per second. The smaller the size you can buy the better. Be sure to buy the necessary batteries to operate all of them. Good batteries. Not dead ones. Do you have that?"

"Got it," Harley said.

"Repeat it."

"Four cassette tape recorders . . ."

"Players. They need not be recorders."

"Okay," Harley said. "Got it. Players. Battery operated. Get fresh batteries. Small size players. Make sure they run at $1\frac{7}{8}$ inches per second."

"That's fine. Now. Underneath the telephone at which you're standing, you will find a key. It's taped to the underside of the shelf. Take it off and hang on to it. You will use it for your final instructions and for the next installment of your payment. Did you find the key?"

"I've got it."

"Okay. Now don't screw things up. In a few days we are going to embarrass the entire government as it's never been embarrassed before. Your participation is vital. Goodbye."

Harley recoiled at the sharp click of the phone in his ear. Then he slammed the telephone onto the hook, snarled "jerkoff," and walked out of the booth to go to a wine shop on his way back to his apartment.

CHAPTER FOURTEEN

"I don't have anything," Remo said for the second time.

"That just won't do." Smith's tone of voice made his usual lemony snarl seem like undiluted saccharin paste.

"Oh, it won't, will it? Well, try this on for size. I don't have anything and I don't think I'm going to get anything."

"Try this one on for size too," Smith said. "You're all, God help us, that we've got. We don't have much time now. "I . . ."

"Smitty," Remo interrupted, "what's the price for a futures contract on hog bellies?"

"Three thousand four hundred and twelve dollars," Smith said, "but . . ."

"What's the exchange rate of Dutch guilders for American dollars?"

"Three point two-seven guilders per dollar. Stop it, will you? We are charged with our biggest single mission and we . . ."

"What's gold selling for?"

"One hundred thirty seven dollars twenty-two cents an ounce." Smith paused. "I presume all this has a point."

"Yeah, it has a point," Remo said. "The point is you've got sixty-three million frigging people on your frigging payroll and you know the market for caterpillar crap in Afghanistan and you know how many pounds of chicken bones the Zulus buy each year to wear in their noses and what they pay for them and you can find out anything and everything and now when it gets sticky, you give the find-out to me. Well, I don't have your damned resources. I'm not good at finding out. I don't know who's going to try to kill the President. I don't know how they're going to try to do it. I don't know how to stop them. And I think they're going to be successful. And I think if you want to stop them you ought to take your far-flung organization and use it and if you can't use it, stuff it, that's what I think."

"All right," Smith said evenly. "Your objections are noted and filed. You've been to the Capitol?"

"Yes. And I didn't find out a thing except that three congressmen are fat and Neil used to work at Colgate's."

"You have no idea how they could attempt an assassination?"

"None at all," said Remo.

"Chiun? What does he think?"

"He thinks it's unusual that there are no roaches in the Capitol."

"That's wonderful," said Smith. His voice would have sounded sarcastic if it hadn't always sounded sarcastic. "That is the best word you have for me?"

"Yeah. If you want anything more, read the Warren Commission report. Maybe they'll tell you something," Remo said.

"Maybe they will at that," Smith said. "I trust you'll keep working?"

"Trust all you want," Remo said.

He hung up and looked angrily at Chiun who was sitting in a lotus position on a red straw mat on the floor. His golden daytime robe was spread gently about him. His eyes were closed and his face serene. He looked so peaceful it seemed as if he might vanish any moment into a mist of wysteria scent.

Chiun raised his hand in Remo's general direction, a silent soft stop sign.

"I am not interested in your problems," he said.

"You're a big help."

"I have told you. You have to find The Hole. That is how this murder attempt . . ."

"Assassination," Remo corrected.

"Wrong," said Chiun. "Assassination is carried out by an assassin. An act of skill, talent, and training. Until I know otherwise it's crude murder. And please stop interrupting. It's rude. Your manners have become unbearable."

"I'm sorry I'm rude. I'm really sorry. Smitty's yelling at me and the President's going to be killed and you're worried that I'm rude."

"A human being should not stop acting like a human being just because some petty annoyances enter his daily life," Chiun said. "At any rate, you must find The Hole. That is how they will try to kill this man of many teeth."

"And where do I find this hole?"

Chiun's eyes widened like those of a jockey who had just found an unexpected opening on the rail. They showed joy at the chance to stick it to Remo.

Remo raised his hand. "Never mind," he said. "I know. I can find The Hole in my head. In my fat stomach. In something or other. Can the insults, Chiun. I've got problems."

Chiun sniffed. "Then find The Hole."

"Leave me alone. I don't need any Eastern philosophy right now."

"Wisdom is always useful. If he paid attention to the coming and going of the sun, the worm wouldn't be eaten by the bird."

"Aaaaah," said Remo in disgust and ran at the wall behind Chiun. His feet hit it, four feet up, and he moved his legs up in a running step, while bringing his head down and around. When his feet were almost at the ceiling and his head almost touching the floor, he did a slow almost lazy flip to land back on his feet.

"Work the corners," Chiun said. He closed his eyes again and gently touched the five fingertips of his left hand to the five fingertips of his right.

"Aaaaah," Remo said again. But he worked the corners, moving up onto a wall as he ran to a corner, running around the corner on the wall, coming down off the wall onto the floor, moving across the room, cutting the room into four triangles, his feet touching the floor only four times for each rosetted circuit of the room.

He was still at it when the knock came on the door.

Remo stopped. Chiun's eyes were closed. Remo did not know how long he had been exercising, whether it was ten minutes or an hour. His heart beat was the same fifty-two it always was at rest, his respiration still twelve breaths a minute. His body was without sweat; he had not perspired for over a year.

A bellboy stood outside the door. He had a white envelope in his hand, a large padded envelope. "This was just delivered for you, sir."

Remo looked at the envelope. It was addressed in felt-tipped printing to his hotel registry name: Remo McArgle. No return address. He felt the envelope. It felt like a book.

He gave it back to the bellhop. "I don't want it," he said.

"There's no charges due on it," the bellhop said.

"Why'd you say that?" Remo asked. "You think I'm poor?"

"No sir. Not in this room. It's just if you don't take it, what'll I do with it? There's no return address."

"Oh, all right. I'll take it." Remo took the envelope back. "Here. For you." He reached into his pocket and fished out a roll of bills and handed them to the bellhop without looking.

The bellhop looked. "Oh, no, sir." He fanned the bills and saw tens, twenties, even a fifty. "You've made a mistake."

"No mistake. You take that. Buy your own hotel. I was poor once and I don't ever want you to think I'm poor. Here. Take my change too." Remo turned his pocket inside out and gave the bellhop several dollars in dimes and quarters, Remo having long ago solved the problem of carrying other kinds of change by simply throwing it all in the street before it had a chance to accumulate.

The bellhop raised his eyebrows. "You sure, sir?"

"I'm sure. Get out of here. I'm working the corners and then I'm going to look for The Hole and sixty-three million people can't find out one little

166

thing and I'm supposed to. Wouldn't it make you mad?"

"It sure would, sir."

"Goodbye," Remo said. Before slamming the door, he yelled out into the hall, "And I'm not poor either."

When the door closed, Chiun said. "You *are* poor. You are a poor substitute for rational man. If the race had depended on you, it would still be sleeping in the forks of trees."

"I don't want to hear about it. I want to read my mail."

Remo opened the padded envelope with the slit of a fingernail, like a bladed paper cutter. Inside was a book:

Summary: The Presidential Commission on the Assassination of President Kennedy.

There was no note. Remo threw the hard-covered blue bound book onto the floor.

"Just what I need," he growled. "Smitty sending me a book to read."

Chiun said, "With all these interruptions it becomes more and more impossible to meditate. First the Mad Emperor on the telephone, then you working the corners with heavy leaden feet, puffing like a chee-chee train . . ."

"Choo choo," said Remo.

"And that boy at the door. Enough is enough." Chiun rose to his feet like a twist of smoke under pressure, released from a wide-topped jar. As he came up he brought the book with him. "What is this document?" he said.

"A report the government made when President Kennedy was murdered."

"Why do they call it 'assassination,' " Chiun

asked, "when it was murder, not an assassination?"

"I don't know," Remo said. "I forgot to ask."

"Have you ever read this book?"

"No. I favor light reading. Schopenhauer. Kant. Like that."

"Who is Schopenhauer and why can't he?"

"Why can't he what?" Remo asked.

"What you just said. Schopenhauer can't."

"Never mind," Remo said.

"You can always improve your mind by reading," Chiun said. "In your case, it may be the only avenue left."

He opened the book and looked inside.

"This is a nice book," he said.

"Glad you like it. Consider it a gift **fro**m me to you. With love."

"That is very thoughtful of you. You are not all bad."

"Enjoy it. I'm going out."

"I will try to endure," Chiun said.

Down in the lobby, Remo looked up the telephone number of the Secret Service. He fished in his slacks for a dime, but his pockets were empty.

He saw the bellboy who had delivered the book to him and motioned him to come over. The boy came slowly, as if fearing Remo had come to his senses and wanted his money back.

"Hey, kid, can you lend me a dime?"

"Yes sir," the boy said. He handed over exactly one dime.

"And I'm not poor," Remo said. "I'll pay it back."

Obviously the Secret Service had not yet caught the full meaning of Washington's new spirit of open people's government because when Remo arrived to talk to someone about a plot to assassinate the President, he was not directed to the office he wanted. Instead he was whisked off to a room where four men demanded to know who he was and what he wanted.

"When did you plan to do it?"

"Do what?" Remo asked.

"Don't get smart, fella."

"Don't worry, I won't. It'd make me too conspicuous around here."

"We'll just have to hold you for a while."

"Look. I'm looking for a guy. He's always popping pills. I don't remember his name, but everybody ought to remember his nervous stomach. I talked to him yesterday."

"You mean Benson?"

"I guess so. I talked to him yesterday with a congressional committee."

"You're with a congressional committee."

"That's right," Remo said.

"Which one?"

"The House Under Committee on Over Affairs. I'm the Middle Secretary."

"I don't know that one."

"Call Benson, will you please?"

When Remo was escorted into Benson's office a few minutes later, the assistant director was swallowing a palmful of pills as if they were salted peanuts and he was in training for a cabinet appointment.

"Hello," the man sputtered as he choked and coughed.

"Drink some water," Remo said. As Benson drank, he said, "I thought Chiun got you off the pills. By talking about the egg."

"He did. I was golden for a day. But today everything started off wrong and before I knew it I was hooked again."

"Stay with it, that's the answer," Remo said. "The first few weeks are the hardest."

"I'm going to. I'm going to try again as soon as I get rid of this pile of papers on my desk."

Remo looked at a foot-high stack of reports and correspondence on the wood-finished metal desk and wanted to shake his head. Benson would never get off the pills because he would never find the time to get off the pills. There would always be too much work, or a too-cranky wife, or too-bad weather. There would always be something to stop him, to put off his plan until tomorrow, and he would just keep on with pills. Better living through chemistry. Better living and faster dying.

"So what can I do for you?" asked Benson, the coughing jag completed.

"You know that the threat has come. The President's supposed to be killed tomorrow."

Benson met Remo's eyes levelly, then nodded. "We know. We're on it. One thing I don't understand is how you know so much about it."

"Congress," Remo said by way of explanation.

"If Congress knew anything about this, it'd be all over the papers by now. Just who are you?"

"That's not important," Remo said. "Just we're on the same side. I want to know more about the payments that you made in the past."

Benson squinted, then shook his head. "I don't think I can give you that," he said.

"If you want, I can have the President of the United States call you and tell you to give me that," Remo said. He met Benson's eyes coldly.

Benson's eyes were bloodshot, the eyes of a man who had gotten early on into the bad habit of working too hard and then found out that bureaucracies searched out such people unerringly and loaded work on them until they collapsed under the pressure. Benson's workload would decrease the day the bureaucracy found out he had been dead for three months.

"You won't have to do that," Benson said. "I guess it won't do any harm to tell you about that." Talking to Remo meant one less phone call he'd have to take, a half-dozen fewer pieces of paper that came across his desk, one less problem to take home. It was a mistake, but the kind made by the overworked. That was the way empires crumbled. Because people became too busy to be careful.

"We sent the tribute money to a bank account in Switzerland," Benson said. "I told you, I think. Walgreen delivered it for us."

"And that's where it died?"

"No. We had it tracked from there, but it went through different accounts to a half-dozen different countries. Mostly in Africa. And eventually it just got lost out and we couldn't ever nail anybody with it."

"No clues? No surmises?"

"None at all," said Benson.

"And you've still got nothing about tomorrow's festivities?" Remo asked.

Benson shook his head. "Somehow," he said, "I get the idea that you're more than just a congressional flunkie."

"That's a possibility," Remo said. "Have you done everything for tomorrow? In the way of protection?"

171

"Everything. Every tree. Every telephone pole. Every manhole cover. Every rooftop within mortar range. Everything. We've done every goddam thing we can, nailed down every loose end we can think of. And somehow I know it's still not enough."

"Maybe we'll struggle through," Remo said, suddenly feeling pity for Benson, and envy for the dedication to his duty that drove him into his destructive overwork.

"You got your best men on this?" Remo asked as he stood and walked toward the door.

Benson was popping an Alka Seltzer into a glass of water. He looked up and nodded. "I'm heading the detail myself."

"Good luck," Remo said.

"Thanks. We're all going to need it," Benson said.

"Maybe."

Osgood Harley had bought the four battery-operated cassette players in an office supply store on K Street. He paid for them with four new fifty-dollar bills. Then, grumbling because the cardboard box was bulky and heavy, he hailed a cab outside the store.

When the driver got to Harley's tenement building, Harley tried to pay with a fifty-dollar bill.

"Can't change that, buddy."

"Don't see too many of these, I suppose," Harley said.

"Not in this neighborhood. What you got that's smaller?"

"You name it."

"A pleasant little five-dollar bill would be nice,"

172

said the cabbie, glancing again at the $3.45 fare on the meter.

"You got it," Harley said. He handed a five-dollar bill to the driver, then waited for his change, which the driver slowly and painstakingly counted out, giving Harley plenty of time to consider the virtues of tipping.

Harley stuffed the change in his pocket without counting it. He had the carton only halfway out of the cab when the driver pulled away.

"Hey, slow down," Harley yelled through the still open door.

"Cheap bastard, screw you and your fifty-dollar bills," the driver called.

He stepped harder on the gas. The cab lurched away. The box of tape players slipped out but Harley caught them before they had a chance to drop hard on the pavement. Then he hoisted them to his chest and still grumbling curses under his breath carried them up to his fourth-floor apartment.

CHAPTER FIFTEEN

Remo knew why the Secret Service men had ulcers, nervous conditions, and the highest rate of early retirement in the federal service.

Because they were asked to do the impossible. It was impossible to try to protect the President. If someone wanted him dead bad enough and was willing to die himself, a kamikaze attack would work.

All the Secret Service could do was to try to protect the President against planned killings, against plots on his life whose motive was something different from blind, unreasoning hate. And they worked at it.

Remo had checked the roofs of all the buildings within sight and shooting distance of the Capitol steps where the President would speak in the morning. The Secret Service had already been there. Remo could see the scuff marks in the tar and gravel roofs where men had been clambering around, inspecting the buildings.

And they had checked the trees and the utility poles and the sewers and the manhole covers. Remo checked them too and found tape seals that the Service had placed over the covers. In the morning they would check them again to make sure they had not been tampered with.

The Secret Service had logged the make and license numbers of all cars parked in the area and run them through federal data banks, against the lists of everyone who had ever made a threat against any President. If one of the cars belonged to somebody with a history of talking about killing the President, they would have scoured the city looking for him, to place him under arrest.

The inspection took Remo the entire night. Chiun had told him to look for The Hole. But where? And what the hell did an ancient Korean legend have to do with an attempt to kill a twentieth-century President? Still, Walgreen had been blown up in Sun Valley. That was the classic use of The Hole by an assassin. And it had worked.

If there was any trouble at the Capitol in the morning, the Secret Service would probably push the President into a car and whisk him the hell out of there. It was inconceivable that the Secret Service would not be sure its cars were secure; that there was nothing planted in them, no bombs, no poison gas. Inconceivable that the escape route from the capitol would not be secured by agents all along the route.

Pink was beginning to streak the low corners of the sky as Remo stood across the street from the Capitol and watched the guards watch the platform from which the President would deliver his speech.

Maybe Chiun was wrong. Maybe the attack on the President would be simple and straightforward, a simple bombing attack. It gave Remo chills. The thought stuck with him that someone could have a damned mortar out there somewhere in the city and could, with reasonable accuracy, plump down a high explosive fragmentation shell in the President's vicinity while he was talking. And Remo could do nothing about it.

Maybe the platform, the speaking platform itself. Who could tell?

Remo moved away from the wall against which he lounged and into the blackness of shadow cast by a tree. He moved, picking his way from shadow to shadow, across the brightly illuminated street and plaza, toward the Capitol steps. The two guards at the platform looked resolutely ahead, toward the streets as if that were the only place trouble could come from. Remo moved to the side of the long steps. At the base of the building, he climbed the wall and let himself lightly over the top railing of the steps.

He was behind the guards now. They did not hear him and did not turn around as he came down the steps from the direction of the Capitol entrance. He slid under the wood and steel platform which cantilevered out over a dozen of the stone steps, and began to inspect the joints where the structure had been put together.

The joints were clean; Remo went over every inch of the underside of the platform. He ran his fingertips over the wooden four-by-fours and the steel piping that gave the structure its strength. He felt the wood for weaknesses that might indicate some kind of load had been placed in it. Nothing.

His fingertips tapped along the pipe very lightly, looking for sound variations that would signal that a hollow steel pipe was no longer hollow. But all the pipes were hollow.

Glints of light were now coming through the

wooden flooring of the platform over his head. Remo could hear the guards on either side of the stand moving heavily from foot to foot. In the silent still of pre-dawn Washington, in which no breeze blew and no puff of air moved, he could smell the meat on their breaths. One had been drinking beer too. The sour smell of fermented grains assaulted Remo's nostrils. And once, he had liked beer.

"Lot of crap this is," one guard said. The accent was pure Pittsburgh, a farmer's twang with the harsh consonants of the city stuck into it like tacks in a board.

"What's that?" the other guard asked.

"What the hell we standing here for all night? What they expect? Termites?"

"I don't know," the other said. The voice was nasal New York. Remo reflected that Washington was one of the few cities in the world that didn't have any distinctive speech pattern of its own. It was filled with drifters and accents from all over. The only change now from ten years earlier was there were a few more people saying "Y'all." And that might all stop in a few hours, Remo thought. The idea made him chilly.

"Maybe they're expecting some trouble or something," New York said.

"If they was, they sure as hell wouldn't be going through with this," Pittsburgh said. "They'd keep the President in the White House and not let him out."

"Yeah. Guess they would at that," said New York. "If they had any sense, anyway."

Remo nodded. That was right. If anybody had any sense they would keep the President in the White House until the danger had passed. To hell with the freedom of the presidency and to hell with what the President had decided he must do. Remo had just made the decisions for the day. The President was staying home.

Remo rolled out from under the platform and was moving again up the steps when he met Viola Poombs coming out of the building. She was smoothing the skirt of her white linen suit.

"Remo," she called. The guards turned to watch them and Remo did not want to run away from her now. He waited on the steps for her to reach him.

"Working overtime?" he asked.

"Yes. And no smart talk from you either," Viola said. "What are you doing here?"

"Just hanging out." He walked down the steps with her.

"Will your Oriental friend really help me with my book?" she asked.

"Sure. It's what we want most in life. Personal publicity."

"Good," Viola said. "Then it'll be a great book and I'll make tons of money."

"And pay tons of taxes."

"Not me," said Viola. "I'll figure out a way to squirrel it away."

They were on the sidewalk now, walking away from the Capitol.

"Oh, that's right," Remo said. "Swiss bank accounts."

They were almost out of eyesight of the guards. Then he would leave this dip.

"Swiss accounts? Kindergarten stuff," Viola said. Where had she heard that, she wondered. "You just wash your money through a Swiss bank, then you transfer it around into a lot of

African accounts . . ." Why did she say that? Why Africa? She knew nothing about Africa. "And it gets lost there and nobody can trace it."

Remo stopped on the street and took Viola's elbows in his hands. He turned to face her. "What do you know about washing money through Swiss banks and African accounts?"

"Nothing. I don't even know why I said that. Why are you looking like that? What'd I say?"

"You must know something about it to talk like that," Remo said. "One of those congressmen you work for. Was it Poopsie who told you that?"

"Poopsie? No. He didn't," Viola said.

"Who then?" asked Remo.

"I don't know. Why?"

"You've got to know. The guy I'm looking for does that with his money. And I've got to find him."

The squeezing by Remo's hands hurt her elbows.

"It's important," he said.

"Let me think. Let go of my elbows. They hurt."

"They'll help you think. Kind of stops the mind from wandering."

She screwed up her face in pain as Remo squeezed.

"Okay, let go. I got it now."

"Who is it?"

"First let go," Viola said.

Remo released her arms.

"Montrofort," she said.

"Montrofort? Who . . ."

"The dwarf with the nice teeth," Viola said. She wondered why she'd said that.

"At Paldor?" Remo said.

Viola nodded. "He told me the other night, about how you do money and everything. He said African banks." It was coming back to her now.

"What'd you say?" Remo asked.

"I said if he touched me, I'd roll him into the fireplace," Viola said.

"Reasonable. You have to do me a favor. Can you take a message to Chiun?"

"Why don't you just telephone him?"

"He has this way of answering phones which involves ripping the wires out of the wall and crushing the instruments to powder."

"All right. I'll do it."

"Go tell Chiun that we know it's Montrofort. Got that so far?"

"I'm not stupid. What's the message?"

"We know it's Montrofort. I'm going to go get him. Tell Chiun to stop the President from coming to the Capitol today."

"How's he going to be able to do that?"

"The first step he'll take will be to tell you I'm an idiot. And then he'll figure out a way to do it. Hurry now. It's important," Remo said. He told Viola the suite number in their hotel, and then turned and ran off down the street to find Sylvester Montrofort.

They had started coming to Osgood Harley's walkup at five o'clock in the morning.

He no longer had 200 friends in what used to be called the peace movement. But he still had twenty. And those twenty had friends. And those friends had friends. And to each of them, Harley gave a camera and instructions, told them that at the least they could keep the cameras and sell them, and told them how much fun it would be to raise a little hell with a presidential speech. Some got cap pistols. To his three closest associates, Harley gave a camera, instructions, and a small tape player, a roll of adhesive tape, and more instructions.

And in the early morning, he was among the group that started to gather in the plaza in front of the Capitol. There wasn't much happening yet. He saw some of his own people. Two guards stood at the speakers' platform watching everybody. The Capitol itself looked empty. Nobody going in or out. The only sign of life was some guy with thick wrists and dead eyes standing on the steps, talking to a woman in a white linen suit with a bust so incredible it made him yearn for the good old days when girls thought the best way to get peace was to give a piece.

The President of the United States had quietly changed his plans the night before. The nerves were getting to him a little. He had not heard from Dr. Smith at CURE. The Secret Service had learned nothing new. He hoped through dinner for a visit from Smith's two field men, Mr. Remo and Mr. Chiun.

But they had not come and so, after dinner he helicoptered to Camp David to spend the night. The next morning he would fly back to Washington, right to the Capitol grounds, for his address.

"Remo is an idiot."

Viola Poombs had found Chiun in the hotel room. He had not answered her knocks on the door, but the door was surprisingly unlocked. Who left hotel room doors unlocked anymore?

Inside she found Chiun sitting on a reed mat,

reading a heavy leather-bound book. He smiled when she entered and closed the book.

"I have found The Hole," he said.

"I guess that's good. Remo says you have to stop the President from speaking today."

"That Remo is an idiot. Where is he now? Why doesn't he do anything himself? Why must I? Remo is an idiot."

"He said you would say that," Viola said.

"He did? Did he say I would say he was a pale piece of pig's ear?"

Viola shook her head.

"Duck droppings?"

She shook her head no again.

"An impossible attempt to make diamonds from river mud?"

"No. He didn't say that," admitted Viola.

"Good. Then I have a few things to tell him myself when he returns. Where is he now?"

"He's gone after Sylvester Montrofort. He said that he's the one."

"One should never trust a man like that," Chiun said.

"You mean a cripple?"

"No. One who smiles so much."

"What did you mean, you found The Hole?" Viola asked.

"It is all here in this book," Chiun said. He pointed to the blue-bound summary of the Warren Commission report. "If Remo knew how to read I would not have to do clerk's work. You find him and tell him that. And tell him that I will do this last thing for him, but none of it has been contracted for, and this will have to be adjusted later. How much am I expected to do? Is it not enough that I have spent ten years trying to teach a pig to whistle? Now I am supposed to make your emperor stay home today. And will Remo want me to do it right? No, he'll say. Don't you dare hurt the emperor, Chiun. Be nice, Chiun, he will say. All right. I will do this last thing. I will go to this ugly white building at number 1600 Philadelphia Avenue..."

"Pennsylvania Avenue?" Viola said.

"They are the same," Chiun said.

"No, they're not."

"I will go there nevertheless to do this thing. But after that, no more Mister Nice Guy. Tell Remo that."

"I will. I will."

"And be sure to put it in your book," Chiun said.

The crowd had doubled and redoubled in only minutes. Now there were more than a thousand persons crowded around the Capitol steps and the small plaza in front of the building, awaiting the arrival of the President. Osgood Harley looked around for faces he recognized. He saw more than a dozen that he knew. But he knew he had more people there than that. He could tell by the new Instamatics hanging from cords around people's necks, scores and scores of them. He smiled to himself and casually patted the tape player he had attached to the inside of his right thigh with adhesive tape, under his baggy khaki pants. Soon now.

The door to Sylvester Montrofort's private office was locked. When Remo stepped on the pressure plate on the receptionist's side of the door, it did not open.

Remo dug his fingers, like wood chisels, into the end of the walnut door, near the lock. His hardened fingertips bit into the polished wood as if it were marshmallow. He curled his fingers, and threw his body back along the direction of the door's slide. The door slipped its lock and slammed open with a shuddering thud.

Remo stepped inside, looked around and then up. Sylvester Montrofort was sitting on a platform behind his desk, but six feet above the floor. He was smiling down at Remo, a broad, even smile, perhaps even more joyful because in his right hand he carried a .44 Magnum. It was pointed at Remo. Behind him, on a wall, was a six- by four-foot television screen. In full color, it showed the crowd gathering at the Capitol.

"What do you want?" Montrofort asked Remo.

"You."

"Why me?" asked Montrofort.

"Because I couldn't find Grumpy, Sneezy, or Doc. You'll have to do. You know goddam well why."

"Well, it's nice that you're here. You can stay and watch the President's speech at the Capitol," Montrofort said.

"The President's not going to be there."

Montrofort's smile did not waver. Nor did the gun pointed at Remo's belly. "You lose, old fella," Montrofort said. "There's his helicopter landing from Camp David."

Remo glanced at the large television projection screen. It was true. The presidential chopper was landing on the Capitol grounds. The side doors opened and the President was coming down the portable steps. Secret Service men swarmed around him as the President briskly stepped off the hundred yards to the Capitol platform where he was going to deliver his speech.

Remo could feel a small sinking sensation in his stomach. Chiun would have gone to the White House, but with the President not there . . . more than likely he would have gone straight back to his hotel room to ponder the cruelties of a world that sent the Master of Sinanju off on a fool's errand. The President was without protection against Montrofort's plan, whatever it was.

Remo looked up again at the dwarf, still seated six feet above the level of the floor, his wheelchair locked into position atop the carpeted platform.

"Why, Montrofort?" Remo asked. "Why not just keep collecting the blackmail?"

"Blackmail's a hard word. Tribute sounds so much better."

"Call it what you want. The blood money. Why not just keep collecting it?"

"Because I have all the money I need. What I want is for them to know that there is a power here . . ." he tapped his forehead with his left forefinger, ". . . that is greater than any defense they can muster. In exactly twelve minutes, this President will be dead. Some poor fool will be hunted down and made out to be the mastermind. And I will be free. And maybe next time I won't ask for tribute. Maybe I'll ask for California. Who knows?"

"You're as loose as lambshit," Remo said. "And you're not going to ask for anything. Dead men don't ask."

He glanced toward the television. The President had passed through the rear of the Capitol building and was coming down the steps toward the speaker's platform. A phalanx of Secret Service men surrounded him. At the top of the steps, Remo could see the Speaker of the House standing, glumly watching. When Remo looked away, Montrofort was staring at him again.

"I'm going to be dead?" he said. "Sorry, bucko, but there are two things wrong with that. W-R-O-N-G. Wrong. I've been living in a dead body all my life. Dead doesn't scare me because I can't get any deader. That's one."

"What's two?" asked Remo.

"I'm the one holding the gun," Montrofort said.

The television set concentrated on the crowd roar now, as they cheered the President who stood on the wooden platform, waving to the audience. His famous smile seemed a little strained to Remo but he was smiling and Remo admired him, for a moment, for his foolish courage. His stupid bravery.

"Don't you know guns are out this year?" Remo told Montrofort. "The beautiful people don't carry them anymore and since you're such a raving beauty, I can't figure you knowing how to use that. How are you going to get the President?"

"I'm not going to get him. He's going to get himself."

"Like Walgreen? Moving into a safe house and have it explode underneath him?"

"Just like that," Montrofort said. "The report on the Kennedy assassination. It tells you in there just how to do it."

The Hole, Remo thought. Chiun had been right.

"Since I'm going to be dead," Remo said, "tell me how."

"Watch and see."

"Sorry, Tom Thumb. I don't have time for

that." The President had started speaking to the crowd. Remo's lips were set hard. Even with Montrofort's plan, he could not get to the Capitol in time to stop it.

Montrofort looked at his wall clock. "Six more minutes."

"You know what?" Remo said.

"What, laddie?"

"You're never going to see it happen."

Remo moved into the room on a run and a roll, heading for the protective overhang of the huge cubic platform that Montrofort sat on.

As he moved, he heard a woman's voice behind him.

"Remo." It was Viola.

He moved toward the platform before turning back to caution Viola away. Atop the platform, Montrofort had swung his wheelchair around to face the door at which Remo had been standing. He squeezed off a shot. The large room resounded with the echoing blast of the heavy charge. The slug caught Viola in the center of her chest. Its force lifted her body and tossed her three feet back into the receptionist's office. Remo had seen mortal wounds. That was one.

He growled, more in frustration than in anger, then coiled his leg muscles and exploded them upward. He was standing on the platform behind Montrofort's wheelchair. The dwarf was trying to spin around, to find Remo to get a shot at him.

Remo pressed his hands against both sides of Montrofort's skull from behind.

"You lose," he said. "L-O-S-E." Montrofort tried to point the gun up over his shoulder. But before his finger could tighten on the trigger, he could hear the sound of cracking. His own skull was cracking under the pressure of Remo's hands. It was as if walnuts were being broken inside his head. The cracks were loud and sharp but there was no pain. Not yet. And then the bones gave way and shards of bone imploded into Montrofort's brain. And then there was pain. Brutal blinding pain that no longer felt as if it were happening to someone or something else.

Remo gave the wheelchair a shove. It catapulted forward off the six-foot-high platform, sailing into the room like a motorcycle stunt man clearing six buses. The chair hit with a heavy metallic thump and it and Montrofort lay in a heap.

Remo did not see it hit: he was at Viola's side.

She was still breathing. Her eyes were open and she smiled when she saw him.

"Chiun said . . ."

"Don't worry about it," Remo said. He looked down at the wound. The front of her linen suit was matted with blood and flesh, a spreading stain already a foot square. In the center of the fabric was a two-inch hole and Remo knew that in the back of Viola's body would be a hole six times that big. Magnums had a way of doing that.

"I worry," she gasped. "Chiun said he'd go to the White House and stop the President."

"It's okay," Remo said. Behind him he heard the President's unrhythmic voice speaking to the crowd at the Capitol.

"Said something else . . ."

"Don't worry," said Remo.

"He said you're an idiot," Viola said. "You're not an idiot. You're nice." She smiled again and her eyes closed. Remo felt the life leave her body as it rested in his arms and he set her gently down on the rug.

Behind him, in Montrofort's office, Remo heard a change in the television sound. The President's voice had stopped. The announcer's voice had cut in.

"Something appears to be going on here," the announcer said.

Remo looked back at the screen covering the side of Montrofort's wall.

The television camera at the Capitol was mounted on a platform, high over the scene. It panned around the crowd and caught the look of confusion on the faces of the thousands who jammed the Capitol steps. The picture seemed to be flickering and Remo realized what it was. Hundreds of people in unison, setting off flashbulbs. In the background, there was the sound of a siren. Remo could make it out. People were looking around to see where the sound came from.

Remo saw that it came from a slack-jawed man on the right side of the crowd. He was wearing floppy khaki trousers and was trying too hard to be casual.

Then there were more sounds. This time of screams and shouts. It came from the left side of the crowd. Remo spotted the man who was the source of the sound. Probably some kind of recording devices, Remo thought. He knew now what was going to happen and here he was on the other side of the city, helpless, unable to do anything. For a fleeting moment, he thought of calling Smith. But even Smitty could do nothing now. It was too late.

The Secret Service men around the President had pinched in closer to him. There was confusion on their faces. Remo recognized the pained look of Assistant Director Benson who had told Remo he would lead the security detail himself.

Then there were more sounds. Cap guns, Remo realized. And then the sound of rifle shots. There was a pause. Then the sound of machine gun fire. The wail of a mortar. Remo could see where the sounds came from. Must be tape recorders on their bodies, he thought.

The Secret Service decided it had waited long enough. The crowd was surging back and forth in confusion that could easily be turned into stampeding panic. The tape-recorded screams gave way to real screams. The recorded gunfire continued. The recorded siren wailed. The cap guns popped.

The Secret Service shielded the President with their bodies and moved him away, up the steps to the Capitol building.

"Not up there," Remo said aloud. "Not up there. That's what he wants you to do. That's The Hole.'

The President of the United States wasn't sure what was happening. He had stopped speaking when the flashbulbs and the sirens had started. And then there were the other sounds. Gun shots. Screams. Somehow they didn't sound real.

He still heard the sounds behind him as he was hustled up the broad Capitol steps by the nine Secret Service men.

Protocol vanished when the President was in danger. The Secret Service was in full control.

"Hurry up, for Christ's sakes," a Secret Service man grumbled at the President. He could feel their bodies pressing against him, their arms around his neck and head, shielding him from sniper fire. But there was no sniper fire.

There was nothing. Just noise.

Through a brief slit in the wall of the bodies of the men in front of him, the President could see the Speaker of the House standing in the entrance to the Capitol. The speaker took two steps down toward him, as if to help. The Secret Service brushed by him without slowing down, propelling the President along as if he were a cranky child, into the Capitol. To safety.

He was going to celebrate by drinking two large bottles of Pepto Bismol on the rocks, Assistant Director Benson of the Secret Service decided. He was the first man in the group leading the President up the steps. It looked to him as if the assassination threat was just so much bullshit. So they set off flashbulbs. So they had screams and sirens and maybe even some firecrackers. Cap guns. So what? Only a few feet more and the President would be safe. And there hadn't been a shot fired. There hadn't been an attempt on his life. Nothing had happened. Only a few more feet to safety.

Remo watched as the presidential phalanx disappeared into the entrance of the Capitol. Another camera mounted at the top of the Capitol stairs was wheeled around and was able to focus inside the building. The light was dim and the picture vague but Remo could make out the President standing inside the building, now out of the line of fire of any sniper outside. But it wasn't going to be a sniper. He wanted to shout.

It was going to be a bomb, controlled by a time clock, and it should be going off any second now.

Then Remo saw another figure. A small figure whirled past the camera only momentarily, just long enough for Remo to see him and recognize him. Around the small figure a red robe swirled. The figure swept through the swarm of Secret Service men as if they were fog, and moved to the President.

It was Chiun.

Remo could see the small Oriental's arm raise and his robe wrap itself around the President and then he was moving the President away from the Capitol entrance, back into a farther corner of the building.

"Attaboy, Chiun, attaboy," Remo told the television.

The Secret Service men followed the President and Chiun. Some drew guns. The Speaker of the House ran after them.

They were all out of the view of the camera now. The camera still focused on the empty Capitol entrance.

And then the explosion came. The front of the building seemed to shudder. Smoke and dust poured out. Rock was blasted loose from inside the entrance and peppered the crowd below the Capitol steps. The screaming now became real. Many ran. Some fell to the ground, trying to find cover.

The television announcer's voice, which had been a wet-palmed attempt at a professional drone, now surrendered to panic.

"There's been an explosion. There's been an explosion. Inside the Capitol where the President is.

We don't know yet if he's been hurt. Oh, the humanity."

The image on the television screen switched back and forth as the director at the studio could not make up his mind what to show. There were shots of the crowd panicking. Then shots of the dust-splashing, smoking entrance to the Capitol. Then more shots of the crowd.

Finally the director backed off to the long overall camera view which showed the crowd and the entrance to the building.

Remo kept watching. He was no longer worried about the President. Chiun had been in the explosion too.

There was some movement in the entranceway to the Capitol and the camera moved in, panning in, zooming in as close as its lens would take it.

And then, standing there in the entranceway, was the President of the United States. He waved to the crowd. Then he smiled.

Next to him Remo saw Assistant Director Benson of the Secret Service. He was throwing up.

CHAPTER SIXTEEN

"Tell Chiun he was right about the roaches." Smith's voice over the telephone came as close to expressing joy as Remo had ever been able to remember hearing.

"You were right about the roaches, Chiun," Remo said. Chiun sat looking out the window of their hotel room. He was wearing a powder blue resting kimono.

He waved his hand over his head in a gesture of disgusted dismissal.

"We checked," Smith said. "Montrofort had a controlling interest in the extermination company working on the Capitol. He had planted gelignite explosive all over the building entrance, covering it up as vermin paste," Smith said. "I guess it was a be-ready-for-anything move and when he decided to kill the President, he just put a timer in it and the damned right-to-the-minute presidential scheduling played right into his hands."

"That's how I figure it too," Remo said.

"Tell Chiun he was very brave in shielding the President that way. And smart to leave in the confusion. No one right now, except the President, really knows who was there and what happened."

"Smitty says you were very brave. And smart," Remo said to Chiun.

"Not smart, stupid," said Chiun.

"Chiun says he's been stupid," said Remo.

"Why?" Smith asked.

"He thinks he's been used. His contract with you doesn't call for being a presidential bodyguard. And he got stiffed on the cabfare from the White House to the Capitol. He doesn't think you'll ever pay him back because everybody knows how cheap you are."

"He'll get it back," said Smith. "That's a promise."

"You'll get it back," Remo said. "That's a promise to you from Smitty, Chiun."

"Emperors promise much," said Chiun. "But promises are such empty things."

"He doesn't believe you, Smitty."

"How much was the fare?" Smith asked.

"Chiun, how much was the cab?"

"Two hundred dollars," Chiun said.

"C'mon, Chiun, you could take a cab to New York for two hundred dollars. You only went to the Capitol."

"I was overcharged," Chiun said. "Everyone takes advantage of my basic good and trusting nature."

"Smitty, he says it cost him two hundred dollars but he's just trying to shake you down," Remo said.

"Tell him I'll give him a hundred," Smith said.

"He'll give you a hundred, Chiun," said Remo.

"Tell him in gold," said Chiun. "No paper."

"In gold, Smitty," said Remo.

195

"Tell him okay. By the way, how did he know there was going to be a bomb set off?"

"Easy. Walgreen was killed by a bomb. It was a dry run. Chiun figured it would be the same. A bomb planted long before the threat was made. Put it in a place where the President would be vulnerable. You sent over that Warren Commission report and Chiun read it. He said the Secret Service stupidly told assassins how to act. The report says the Secret Service, in cases of danger to the President, first protects him and then moves him away to the nearest safe place. That obviously had to be right inside the Capitol."

"Obviously," Smith said drily. "If it was so obvious, why didn't I think of it? Or the Secret Service?"

"That's easy," said Remo.

"Why?" said Smith.

"You're not the Master of Sinanju."

"No, that's true," Smith said after a pause. "Anyway, the President would like to thank both of you."

"The President says thanks, Chiun," Remo called out.

"I do not want and will not accept his thanks," Chiun said.

"Chiun doesn't want his thanks," Remo told Smith.

"Why not?"

"The way he figures it the President owes him a new robe. The other one was ripped in the blast."

"We'll get him a new robe."

"Chiun, Smitty says he'll get you a new robe. How much was that one worth?"

"Nine hundred dollars," said Chiun.

"He says nine hundred dollars," said Remo.

"Tell him I'll give him a hundred."

"He'll give you a hundred, Chiun," said Remo.

"I will take it just this one time. But then . . .
no more Mister Nice Guy," Chiun said.

EXECUTIONER 9: VEGAS VENDETTA
by DON PENDLETON

Enraged and embarrassed by the memories of New York and Chicago, the organized crime syndicate is attempting to marshal its forces for a massive counterblow to end the Bolan menace once and for all. The invisible tentacles of the mob's empire reach into every level of society and there's no sanctuary, no sure ally for Mack Bolan in his all-consuming mission to eradicate his enemy – the Mafia.

So, 'get that goddamn Bolan' becomes the battle cry on that desert oasis of greenbacks and neon called Las Vegas . . . and the chips fly as the Executioner loads his dice for one of the wildest games that town has ever seen – a game in which the Mafia learns The Executioner plays for keeps!

0 552 11108 2   75p

EXECUTIONER 10: CARIBBEAN KILL
by DON PENDLETON

The police in thirty states are on the lookout for him. The FBI is on his trail. He's on the VIP list at Interpol. There's virtually no law enforcement agency that isn't familiar with his name, and his game.

But the people most anxious to put him out of business are on the other side of the law – that organized cartel of crime and corruption called the Mafia.

And Bolan's sole purpose in life is to extinguish every trace of the Mafia . . . without the FBI, the police, the courts, or anyone else, if need be . . .

Impossible? Yes. But Bolan's doing it. In this chapter of his [w]ay book, The Executioner invades the Mafia strongholds [of the Ca]ribbean, and although the odds aren't in his favour, all [a]re.

0 552 111   75p